W9-BAL-972

WHITES

WHITES

Stories by
NORMAN RUSH

ALFRED A. KNOPF  NEW YORK 1986

THIS IS A BORZOI BOOK
PUBLISHED BY ALFRED A. KNOPF, INC.

Copyright © 1984, 1985, 1986 by Norman Rush

All rights reserved under International and Pan-American
Copyright Conventions. Published in the United States by
Alfred A. Knopf, Inc., New York, and simultaneously in
Canada by Random House of Canada Limited, Toronto.
Distributed by Random House, Inc., New York.

The following stories have been published previously,
some of them in slightly different form: "Official Americans," *The New Yorker*, Feb. 10, 1986; "Thieving," *Grand
Street*, Winter 1985; "Instruments of Seduction," *The Paris
Review*, Autumn 1984; "Near Pala," *The New Yorker*, May
7, 1984; "Bruns," *The New Yorker*, April 4, 1983.

Library of Congress Cataloging-in-Publication Data

Rush, Norman.
Whites: stories.

Contents: Bruns—Near Pala—Thieving—[etc.]
1. Botswana—Fiction. 2. Whites—Botswana—Fiction.
I. Title.
PS3568.U727W47   1986   813'.54   85-45598
ISBN 0-394-54471-4

Manufactured in the United States of America

A NOTE ON THE TYPE

This book was set in a digitized version of Bodoni Book, a type-
face named after the celebrated printer and type designer Giam-
battista Bodoni (1740–1813).

Composed by Graphic Composition, Inc., Athens,
Georgia. Printed and bound by Fairfield Graphics,
Fairfield, Pennsylvania. Typography and
binding design by Tasha Hall.

For Elsa, beautiful and good,
perfect friend, with gratitude

CONTENTS

WHITES

BRUNS

Poor Bruns. They hated him so much it was baroque. But then so is Keteng baroque, everything about it.

Probably the Boers were going to hate Bruns no matter what. Boers run Keteng. They've been up there for generations, since before the Protectorate. When independence came, it meant next to nothing to them. They ignored it. They're all citizens of Botswana, but they are Boers underneath forever, really unregenerate. Also, in Keteng you're very close to the border with South Africa. They still mostly use rands for money instead of pula. Boers slightly intrigue me. For a woman, I'm somewhat an elitist, and hierarchy always interests me. I admit these things. The Boers own everything in Keteng, including the chief. They wave him to the head of the queue for petrol, which he gets for free, naturally, just like the cane liquor they give him. They own the shops. Also they think they really know how to manage the Bakorwa, which actually they do. You have to realize that the Bakorwa have the reputation of being the most violent and petulant tribe in the country, which is about right. All the other tribes say so. And in fact the Boers do get along with them. In fact, the original whites in Keteng—that would be the Vissers, Du Toits, Pieterses . . . seven families altogether—were all rescued by the Bakorwa when their ox wagons broke down in the desert when they were trekking somewhere. They started out as bankrupts and now they own the place. It's so feudal up there you cannot conceive. That is, it has been until now.

I know a lot about Keteng. I got interested in Keteng out of boredom with my project. Actually, my project collapsed. My thesis adviser at Stanford talked me into my topic anyway, so it wasn't all that unbearable when it flopped. At certain moments I can even get a certain vicious satisfaction out of it. Frankly, the problem is partly too many anthropologists in one small area. We are thick on the ground. And actually we hate each other. The problem is that people are contaminating one another's research, so hatred is structural and I don't need to apologize. At any rate, I was getting zero. I was supposed to be showing a relationship between diet and fertility among the Bakorwa up near Tswapong, in the hills. The theory was that fertility would show some seasonality because the diet in the deep bush was supposedly ninety per cent hunting-gathering, which would mean sharp seasonal changes in diet content. But the sad fact is you go into the middle of nowhere and people are eating Simba chips and cornflakes and drinking Castle lager. The problem is Americans, partly. Take the hartebeest domestication project, where they give away so much food and scraps and things that you have a kind of permanent beggar settlement outside the gate. And just to mention the other research people you have encumbering the ground—you have me, you have the anthropologists from the stupid Migration Study and the census, and you have people from some land-grant college someplace following baboons around. By the way, there were several baboon attacks on Bakorwa gathering firewood around Keteng, which they blame on the Americans for pestering the baboons. Or Imiricans, as the Boers would say. America gets the blame.

The other thing is that Keteng is remote. It's five hours from the rail line, over unspeakable roads, through broiling-hot empty thornveld. In one place there's no road and you just creep over red granite swells for a kilometer, following a little line of rocks. So the Boers got used to doing what they wanted, black government or not. They still pay their farm labor in sugar and salt and permission to crawl underneath their cows and suck fresh milk. It is baroque. So I got interested in Keteng and started weekending. At my project site, camping was getting uncomfortable, I should mention, with strange figures hanging around my perimeter. Nobody did anything, but it makes you nervous. In Keteng I can always get a room from the sisters at the mission hospital and a bath instead of washing my armpits under my shirt because you never know who's watching.

The place I stay when I descend into Keteng is interesting and is one reason I keep going back. I can see everything from the room the sisters give me. The hospital is up on the side of a hill, and the sisters' hostel is higher than that, on the very top. My room is right under the roof, the second story, where there's a water tank and therefore a perpetual sound of water gurgling down through pipes, a sound you get famished for in a place so arid. Also, in tubs on the roof they have vines growing that drape down over the face of the building, so you have this green-curtain effect over your window. The sisters have a little tiny enclosed locked-up courtyard where they hang their underthings to dry, which is supposed to be secret and sacrosanct, which you can see into from my room. You can also see where Bruns stayed— a pathetic bare little shack near the hospital with gravel around the stoop and a camp stool so he could sit in the sun and watch his carrots wither. At the foot of the hill the one street in Keteng begins at the hospital gate and runs straight to the chief's court at the other end of town. Downtown amounts to a dozen one-story buildings—shops—with big houses behind them. You can see the Bakorwa wards spreading away from the center of Keteng—log kraals, mud rondavels with thatch, mostly, although cement-block square houses with sheet-metal roofs held down by cobbles are in-filtrating the scene. Sometimes I think anthropology should be considered a form of voyeurism rather than a science, with all the probing into reproductive life and so forth we do. I'm voyeuristic. I like to pull my bed up to the window and lie there naked, studying Keteng. Not that the street life is so exotic. Mostly it's goats and cattle. I did once see a guy frying a piece of meat on a shovel. The nuns have really hard beds, which I happen to prefer.

Poor Bruns. The first thing I ever heard about him was that there was somebody new in Keteng who was making people as nervous as poultry, as they put it. That's an Afrikaans idiom. They meant Bruns. He was a volunteer from some Netherlands religious outfit and a conscientious objector like practically all the Dutch and German volunteers are. He was assigned to be the fleet mechanic at the mission hospital. He was a demon mechanic, it turned out, who could fix any-thing. Including the X-ray machine, for example, which was an old British Army World War I field unit, an antique every-body had given up on. Of course, what do the Boers care, because when they get even just a little cut it's into the Cessna and over the border into the Republic to Potgieters-rust or even Pretoria. But other people were ecstatic. Bruns was truly amazing. People found out. A few of the Bakorwa farmers have tractors or old trucks, and Bruns, being hyper-Christian, of course started fixing them up for free in his spare time. On Saturdays you'd see Bakorwa pushing these old wrecks, hordes of them pushing these three or four old wrecks toward Keteng for Bruns. So, number one, right away that made Bruns less than popular around Du Toit's garage. Du Toit didn't like it. It even got a little mean, with some of Bruns's tools disappearing from his workroom at the hospital until he started really locking things up.

    The other thing that fed into making people nervous right

away was Bruns physically. He was very beautiful, I don't
know how else to put it. He was very Aryan, with those pale-
blue eyes that are apparently so de rigueur for male movie
stars these days. He had a wonderful physique. At some
point possibly he had been a physical culturist, or maybe it
was just the effect of constant manual work and lifting. Also
I can't resist mentioning a funny thing about Boer men. Or,
rather, let me back into it: there is a thing with black African
men called the African Physiological Stance, which means
essentially that men, when they stand around, don't bother
to hold their bellies in. It might seem like a funny cultural
trait to borrow, but Boer men picked it up. It doesn't look so
bad with blacks because the men stay pretty skinny, usually.
But in whites, especially in Boers, who run to fat anyway, it
isn't so enthralling. They wear their belts underneath their
paunches, somewhat on the order of a sling. Now consider
Bruns strictly as a specimen walking around with his nice
flat belly, a real waist, and, face it, a very compact nice little
behind, and also keep in mind that he's Dutch, so in a
remote way he's the same stock as the Boer men there, and
the contrast was not going to be lost on the women, who are
another story. The women have nothing to do. Help is thick
on the ground. They get up at noon. They consume bales of
true-romance magazines from Britain and the Republic, so
incredibly crude. They do makeup. And they can get very
flirtatious in an incredibly heavy-handed way after a couple
of brandies. Bruns was the opposite of flirtatious. I wonder
what the women thought it meant. He was very scrupulous
when he was talking to you—it was nice. He never seemed
to be giving you ratings on your secondary sex characteris-
tics when he was talking to you, unlike everybody else. He
kept his eyes on your face. As a person with large breasts
I'm sensitized on this. Boer men are not normal. They think
they're a godsend to any white woman who turns up in this
wilderness. Their sex ideas are derived from their animals.

I've heard they just unbanned *Love Without Fear* in South Africa this year, which says something. The book was published in 1941.

On top of that, the Dutch-Boer interface is so freakish and tense anyway. The Dutch call Afrikaans "baby Dutch." Boers are a humiliation to the Dutch, like they are their ids set free in the world or something similar. The Dutch Parliament keeps almost voting to get an oil boycott going against South Africa.

Also it wasn't helpful that Bruns was some kind of absolute vegetarian, which he combined with fasting. He was whatever is beyond lactovegetarian in strictness. You have never seen people consume meat on the scale of the Boers. As a friend of mine says, Boers and meat go together like piss and porcelain. Biltong, sausages, any kind of meat product, pieces of pure solid fat—they love meat. So there was another rub.

Bruns was so naïve. He apparently had no idea he was coming to live in a shame culture. Among the Bakorwa, if you do something wrong and somebody catches you, they take you to the customary court and give you a certain number of strokes with a switch in public. They wet it first so it hurts more. This is far from being something whites thought up and imposed. It's the way it is. The nearest regular magistrate is—where? Bobonong? Who knows? Bakorwa justice is based on beatings and the fear of beatings and shame, full stop. It's premodern. But here comes Bruns wearing his crucifix and wondering what is going on. The problem was he had an unfortunate introduction to the culture. You could call wife beating among the Bakorwa pretty routine. I think he saw an admission to the hospital related to that. Also he himself was an ex-battered child, somebody said. I'm thinking of setting up a course for people who get sent here. I can give you an example of the kind of thing people should know about and not think twice about. The manager of the butchery in one of the towns caught two women shoplifting and he made them stand against the wall while he whipped them with an extension cord instead of calling the police. This shamed them and was probably effective and they didn't lose time from work or their families. You need anthropologists to prepare people for the culture here. Bruns needed help. He needed information.

Bruns belonged to some sect. It was something like the people in England who jump out and disrupt fox hunts. Or there was a similar group, also in England, of people who were interposing themselves between prizefighters, to stop prizefighting. Bruns was from some milieu like that. I think he felt like he'd wandered into something by Hieronymus Bosch which he was supposed to do something about.

The fact is that the amount of fighting and beating there is in Bakorwa culture is fairly staggering to a person at first. Kids get beaten at school and at home, really hard sometimes. Wives naturally get beaten. Animals. Pets. Donkeys. And of course the whole traditional court process, the *kgotla*, is based on it. I think he was amazed. Every Wednesday at the *kgotla* the chief hears charges and your shirt comes off and you get two to twenty strokes, depending. Then there's the universal recreational punching and shoving that goes on when the locals start drinking. So it's not something you can afford to be sensitive about if you're going to work here for any length of time.

Bruns decided to do something. The first thing he tried was absurd and made everything worse.

He started showing up at the *kgotla* when they were giving judgment and just stood there watching them give strokes. He was male, so he could get right up in the front row. I understand he never said anything, the idea being just to be a sorrowful witness. I guess he thought it would have some effect. But the Bakorwa didn't get it and didn't care. He was welcome.

Maybe I'm just a relativist on corporal punishment. Our own wonderful culture is falling apart with crime, more than Keteng is, and you could take the position that substituting imprisonment for the various kinds of rough justice there used to be has only made things worse. Who knows if there was less crime when people just formed mobs in a coopera-tive spirit and rode people out of town on a rail or horse-whipped them, when that was the risk you were running rather than plea bargaining and courses in basket weaving or some other fatuous kind of so-called rehabilitation? I don't.

Bruns convinced himself that the seven families were to blame for all the violence—spiritually to blame at least. He was going to ask them to do something about it, take some kind of stand, and he was going to the center of power, Deon Du Toit.

There's some disagreement as to whether Bruns went once to Du Toit's house or twice. Everybody agrees Du Toit wasn't home and that Bruns went in and stayed, however many times he went, stayed talking with Marika, Du Toit's slutty wife. The one time everybody agrees on was at night. Bruns started to turn away when the maid told him Du Toit wasn't there. But then somehow Bruns was invited in. That's established. Then subsequently there was one long after-noon encounter, supposedly.

Bruns was going to blame the families for everything—for making money off liquor, which leads to violence, for doing nothing about violence to women and not even appear-ing in *kgotla* for women who worked for them when they were brutalized by their husbands or boyfriends, for cor-rupting the chief, who was an incompetent anyway, for doing nothing about conditions at the jail. I can generate this list out of my own knowledge of Bruns's mind: everything on it is true. Finally there was something new he was incensed about. The drought had been bad and Du Toit had just started selling water for three pula a drum. You know a drought is bad when cattle come into town and bite the brass taps off cisterns. A wildebeest charged an old woman carrying melons and knocked her down so it could get the moisture in the melons.

We know what Du Toit did when he came back and found out Bruns had been there. First he punched the housemaid, Myriad Gofetile (her twin sister also works for Du Toit), for letting Bruns in or for not telling him about it, one or the other. And Marika wasn't seen outside the house for a while, although the Boers usually try not to mark their women where it shows when they beat them.

Those are two people I would love to see fighting, Deon and Marika Du Toit, tooth and nail. It would be gorgeous. Both of them are types. He's fairly gigantic. Marika has skin like a store dummy's. She's proud of it. She's one of those people who are between twenty-five and forty but you can't tell where. She has high cheekbones you can't help envying, and these long eyes, rather Eurasian-looking. She wears her hair like a fool, though—lacquered, like a scoop around her head. Her hair is yellowish. She hardly says anything. But she doesn't need to because she's so brilliant with her cigarette, smoking and posing.

Deon was away hunting during the time or times Bruns visited. The inevitable thing happened, besides beating up on his household, when Deon found out. This was the day he got back, midmorning. He sent a yard boy to the hospital with a message to the effect that Bruns is ordered to drop whatever he's doing and come immediately to see Deon at the house.

Bruns is cool. He sends back the message that he's engaged on work for the hospital and regrets he isn't free to visit.

So that message went back, and the yard boy comes back with a new command that Bruns should come to Du Toit's at tea, which would be at about eleven. Bruns sends the message back that he doesn't break for tea, which was true.

Suddenly you have Deon himself materializing in the hospital garage, enraged, still covered with gore from hauling game out of his pickup. He had shot some eland.

"You don't come by my wife when I am away!" He ended up screaming this at Bruns, who just carried on fixing some vehicle.

He now orders Bruns to come to his house at lunch, calling him a worm and so on, which was apropos Bruns being a pacifist.

Bruns took the position that he had authority over who was present in the garage and ordered Du Toit to leave.

Then there was a stupid exchange to the effect that Bruns would come only if Du Toit was in actual fact inviting him to a meal at noon.

Throughout all this Bruns is projecting a more and more sorrowful calmness. Also, everything Bruns says is an aside, since he keeps steadily working. Deon gets frantic. The sun is pounding down. You have this silent chorus of Africans standing around. There is no question but that they are loving every moment.

It ends with Deon telling Bruns he had better be at his house at noon if he expects to live to have sons.

Of course, after the fact everybody wanted to know why somebody didn't intervene.

Bruns did go at lunchtime to Deon's.

The whole front of Deon's place is a screened veranda he uses for making biltong. From the street it looks like red laundry. There are eight or nine clotheslines perpetually hung with rags of red meat turning purple, air-drying. This is where they met. Out in the road you had an audience of Bakorwa pretending to be going somewhere, slowly.

Meat means flies. Here is where the absurd takes a hand. Deon comes onto the porch from the house. Bruns goes onto the porch from the yard. The confrontation is about to begin. Deon is just filling his lungs to launch out at Bruns when the absurd thing happens: he inhales a fly. Suddenly you have a farce going. The fly apparently got rather far up his nostril. Deon goes into a fit, stamping and snorting. He's in a state of terror. You inhale a fly and the body takes over. Also you have to remember that there are certain flies that fly up the nostrils of wildebeests and lay eggs that turn into maggots that eat the brains of the animals, which makes them gallop in circles until they die of exhaustion. Deon has seen this, of course.

The scene is over before it begins. Deon crashes back into his living room screaming for help. It is total public humiliation. The Bakorwa see Bruns walk away nonchalantly and hear Du Toit thrashing and yelling.

Marika got the fly out with tweezers, I heard. By then Bruns was back at work.

Here is my theory of the last act. Deon's next move was inevitable—to arrange for a proxy to catch Bruns that same night and give him a beating. For symbolic and other reasons, it had to be one of the Bakorwa. At this point both Bruns and Deon are deep in the grip of the process of the Duel, capital D. Pragmatically, there would be no problem for Deon in getting one of the Bakorwa to do the job and probably even take the blame for it in the unlikely event he got caught. This is not to say there was no risk to Deon, because there was, some. But if you dare a Boer to do something, which is undoubtedly the way Deon perceived it, he is lost. An example is a man who was dared to kiss a rabid ox on the lips, at the abattoir in Cape Town. It was in the *Rand Daily Mail*. By the way, the point of kissing the ox on the lips is that it gives rabies its best chance of getting directly to your brain. So he did it. Not only that, he defaulted on the course of rabies injections the health department was frantically trying to get him to take. Here is your typical Boer folk hero. Add to that the Duel psychology, which is like a spell that spreads out and paralyzes people who might otherwise be expected to step in and put a stop to something so weird. Still, when someone you know personally like Bruns is found dead, it shocks you. I had cut this man's hair.

I'm positive two things happened the last night, although the official version is that only one did.

The first is that Deon sent somebody, a local, to beat Bruns up. When night falls in Keteng it's like being under a rock. There's no street lighting. The stores are closed. The whites pull their curtains. Very few Bakorwa can afford candles or paraffin lamps. It can seem unreal, because the Bakorwa are used to getting out and about in the dark and you can hear conversations and deals going down and so on, all in complete blackness. They even have parties in the dark where you can hear *bojalwa* being poured and people singing and playing those one-string tin-can violins. There was no moon that night and it was cloudy.

Bruns would often go out after dinner and sit on one of the big rocks up on the hill and do his own private vespers. He'd go out at sunset and sit there into the night thinking pure thoughts. He had a little missal he took with him, but what he could do with it in the dark except fondle it I have no idea.

So I think Bruns went out, got waylaid and beaten up as a lesson, and went back to his hut. I think the point of it was mainly just to humiliate him and mark him up. Of course, because of his beliefs, he would feel compelled just to endure the beating. He might try to shield his head or kidneys, but he couldn't fight back. He would not be in the slightest doubt that it was Bakorwa doing it and that they had been commissioned by Du Toit. So he comes back messed up, and what is he supposed to do?

Even very nice people find it hard to resist paradox. For example, whenever somebody who knows anything about it tells the story of poor Bruns, they always begin with the end of the story, which is that he drowned, their little irony being that of course everybody knows Botswana is a desert and Keteng is a desert. So poor Bruns, his whole story and what he did is reduced to getting this cheap initial sensation out of other people.

As I reconstruct the second thing that happened, it went like this: Bruns wandered back from his beating and possibly went into his place with the idea of cleaning himself up. His state of mind would have to be fairly terrible at this point. He has been abused by the very people he is trying to champion. At the same time, he knows Du Toit is responsible and that he can never prove it. And also he is in the grip of the need to retaliate. And he is a pacifist. He gets an idea and slips out again into the dark.

They found Bruns the next morning, all beaten up, drowned, his head and shoulders submerged in the watering trough in Du Toit's side yard. The police found Deon still in bed, in his clothes, hung over and incoherent. Marika was also still in bed, also under the weather, and she also was marked up and made a bad exhibit. They say Deon was struck dumb when they took him outside to show him the body.

Here's what I see. Bruns goes to Deon's, goes to the trough and plunges his head underwater and fills his lungs. I believe he could do it. It would be like he was beaten and pushed under. He was capable of this. He would see himself

striking at the center of the web and convicting Du Toit for a
thousand unrecorded crimes. It's self-immolation. It's non-
violent.

Deon protested that he was innocent, but he made some
serious mistakes. He got panicky. He tried to contend he
was with one of the other families that night, but that story
collapsed when somebody else got panicky. Also it led to
some perjury charges against the Vissers. Then Deon
changed his story, saying how he remembered hearing some
noises during the night, going out to see what they were,
seeing nothing, and going back in and to bed. This could be
the truth, but by the time he said it nobody believed him.

The ruin is absolute. It is a real Götterdämmerung. Deon is
in jail, charged, and the least he can get is five years. He
will have to eat out of a bucket. The chief is disgraced and
they are discussing a regency. Bruns was under his protection, formally, and all the volunteer agencies are upset. In
order to defend himself the chief is telling everything he can
about how helpless he is in fact in Keteng, because the real
power is with the seven families. He's pouring out details,
so there are going to be charges against the families on other
grounds, mostly about bribery and taxes. Also, an election
is coming, so the local Member of Parliament has a chance
to be zealous about white citizens acting like they're outside
the law. Business licenses are getting suspended. Theunis
Pieters is selling out. There's a new police compound going
up and more police coming in. They're posting a magistrate.

There is ruin. It's perfect.

NEAR PALA

Here the road was a soft red trough. In a Land-Rover laboring along it were four whites, the men in front, the women in back. The landscape was desolate but neat: dry plains, the grass cropped short, small and scattered thorn trees, no deadfall anywhere, late-afternoon light the color of glue.

The men had an acoustic advantage. In the front seat, especially when the Land-Rover was in first or second gear, they could, by leaning slightly forward, talk without being heard in the back. Or they could lean back and monitor or enter conversations proceeding behind them. They began discussing bonuses and leaned forward.

The woman seated behind the driver was discussing her pregnancy, wearily. "Tess, we must leave it," she said. "I'm so tired of my pregnancies as a topic. I'll tell you about Greece. I adored it, and he"—she gestured toward the driver—"loathed it." She waited for something.

She said, "Gareth, did you not loathe Greece?"

"What?" he asked, and then, before she could repeat her question, said, "Yes, Nan."

"There you have it. I adored it, he loathed it. For Gareth there is only one perfect spot: home—Sussex. So that all travel that is not Sussex is just willful. He hated things, Tess, that were so silly, like the Greeks hissing for taxis, which is simply their custom. And in Crete it was the hot-water schedule—an hour in the morning and another before supper, so we must always be poised to race back so as not to miss it. And the pillows were 'sandbags.' They *were* bad. There he had a point. I grant him that."

"We never go to Greece," Tess said.

"Well, you must. But what I truly think is, *we* should. I would rather not go with a man again, or at least not with Gareth, we are so ill-matched for that country. He agrees." Again she listened toward the front. She went on, "I irritated him no end. Item: I thought it was clever to refer to tavernas, places you eat, as though the Greek letters should just be read right off as sort of English, so I called them 'tabepnas.' I had to stop. Not amusing after all. Well. But every time we would see two women traveling together—this was Crete— he would say, 'Well, well, they must be on their way to Lesbos, where it all began.' And I said nothing—not once. Then the fortresses, or 'fortetsas.' They are on headlands, very high, walled about, beautiful, overlooking the blue sea. There were sieges lasting generations. Cooped in, but they could look at the Aegean. So beautiful. But I was saying: On the top, there are date palms, old gardens still growing, graves, mosques. All these different conquerors left different artifacts, you see, and I just wanted to wander at will. But Gareth had it that straight off we must walk all round the perimeter to get a 'sense,' as he said, and only then could one wander at will. So it was. *Placet.* Drive gently, Gareth, we are tipping."

"I adore Cape Town," Tess said. "Botswana is so dry."

"But Greece! We could organize it, Tess, and it is so much the reverse of life at the mine. I mean, the mine is all right. And Cape Town— All right, you go down there, I accept that it's beautiful, but it's far from one hundred per cent the reverse of the mine. I mean, everywhere in South Africa the whites are on compounds, too, but armed and that. One wants something totally unlike—not South Africa!"

"Greece sounds lovely. Would you take the new baby?"

"I forgot."

Gareth said sharply to the women that someone should please hand the water bottle forward to Tom. It was done.

Nan said to Tess, "Truly, one comes to dislike the medical profession. Now I must deal with them again. Coming back here to Botswana from holiday, it was so strange and nice. We were in the plane, coming low over the land. I was happy to see Botswana again. It was so strange, Tess—the country seemed like a poor relation, someone nice who refuses gifts at first, someone you like. This country is so poor. We were flying low over it. And then all I could think of was our friend the peerless Dr. Hartogs, who said that from the air the country looks as if it has ringworm. He was saying that the brush fencing round the family rondavels and kraals looks like that. It spoiled it."

"We love the sea," Tess said. "Give us four days and we make straight for Durban. Durban isn't nice, but it has the sea to put your feet in."

"You'll be singing a different tune about Hartogs when your day comes," Gareth said over his shoulder.

Tess said, "Nowadays whenever I am on paved road I never take it for granted. Even in U.K. I *enjoy* it, just the being on it. Even here, when you get to the paved roads, bad as they are, I just say thank God to myself. I hate these spoors. And why do they call these tire ruts spoors, does anyone know?"

Tom said, "We put in the roads and they don't maintain them, do they? They think a road is a thing like your fingernail—chip it and it grows back. Well, they're wrong, aren't they?"

Gareth slowed. They were approaching a narrow concrete-slab bridge over a gully. There was no more than a yard of clearance on either side of the vehicle. The stream-bed beneath the slab was baked sand pocked with hoofmarks. They crossed safely. The bushes beside the road were plated with red dust.

They passed a small settlement and the men began to laugh. An imposing thorn tree overhanging a shed at the roadside was clotted with paper refuse—streamers of toilet tissue caught in the spines.

Nan said, "It's unfair. We bring in all these metal and plastic things and bottles that don't decay. In the old times, they could leave anything about and it was organic—it would decay or be eaten. Even as it is, the goats eat a lot of the plastic. Look at the courtyards, Tess. They are as neat as you like. They sweep them morning and evening."

"Yes, everything goes into the lane," Gareth said.

"They aren't wasteful," Nan said, in a voice made light. "Every bit of rag they can get they make something with. They make shifts out of maize sacks. They will ask you for your rags and they are so grateful—"

"Hallo! Nan, don't look on the right! Dead beast." Gareth was peremptory.

Nan did as she was told. The men looked. On the bank was the corpse of a heifer, fresh. Dogs or jackals had been at work. There was movement in the brush adjacent.

"Third one this trip," Tom said. "This drought is red hell."

Gareth nodded. He related something that Hartogs, who was a great hunter, had told him. Animals were being driven mad with thirst and were fighting over carrion. There was some zoological protocol between vultures and jackals that was breaking down. The jackals were supposed to withdraw when the birds came, but lately they were staying and fighting. Hartogs had witnessed a magnificent fight. Gareth described it until Nan asked him to stop.

Nan said to Tess, but projecting for the benefit of the front, "Truly, are we so superior as we think? I wonder a little. When we first moved in at the mine, we did something at the house so stupid I am still in pain. There were two pawpaw trees growing side by side by the house, one thriving with nice big pawpaws on it and the other sick-looking and leafless—dead-looking. Well, we thought it was plain what we should do: take down the dead tree. So we hauled and pushed on the trunk of the poor tree and strained and pulled it over—uprooted it, Gareth and myself. It was his idea: we must just straight off do this, get it over. Then, with the crash, the servants come out. They had funny looks on. Dineo said, so quietly, 'Oh, Mma, you have killed the male.' We didn't understand. It seems the pawpaw grow in pairs, couples, male and female. The male tree looks like a phallus—no foliage to it, really. The female needs the male in order to bear. They take years to reach the height ours had. Then the female died. The staff had been eating pawpaws from our tree for years. It was a humiliation."

"Bit ancient times by now, isn't it?" Gareth said angrily.

"So sorry," Nan said.

They saw a woman standing at the edge of a strip of cultivated land, a mealie patch. A baby was bound to her back with a blanket.

Nan resumed, in the same projecting voice, "And these blankets, let me just mention. These blankets they tie their children to them with. One sees the babies in the hot season and they are sweating and drenched. And I know from the sisters that quite a lot of them get pneumonia and die of it, when they shouldn't. Why, do you think? I say because of acrylics. That's all they can get nowadays. The acrylics don't

breathe. Of course, in the old times they used skins, or if
they bought blankets they were wool. But we bring them
marvelous cheap acrylics, make them very cheap and drive
out the wool, and their children are perishing. Try to buy a
wool blanket today at any price in this part of the world."

Gareth half faced the back. "Might I ask where you have
the least proof of that? You don't know a bloody thing about
it. We can't set a foot right if we're white, can we? Regular
litany with you, Nan. You're becoming tiresome!"

"Could you possibly just carry on driving and not over-
turning? Let the women talk, Gareth. No, I have no proof,
sorry. Now watch him start racing."

Tom and Gareth began talking about crime. They agreed that
the situation was getting out of hand.

Tom said, "You know, they have some of those road-
contract chaps billeted in the Shangule Hotel to this day, the
housing they promised is still not ready. Well, I talked to
one of them. Well, you know how the hotel is, just by the
railroad station. Train comes in twelve at night and stops for
five minutes. So what happens? Every night at twelve—*pum
pum pum*, you have these villains bounding down the hall-
ways, footsteps, rattling door handles one after another just
to see if they're unlocked, by chance. Then comes a shout
that the train is going, and *pum pum pum*, everybody pelts
back and all aboard. Every night of the week without fail—
set your watch to it. Life in the metropolis of Shangule."

Tess began complaining to Nan about stealing. "The
stealing is getting terrible, really."

"I know they steal," Nan said. "I think I should steal,
too, in their place. No, I mean this, Tess. I heard a story.
Two American Peace Corps women staying in a rondavel in
Serowe. Middle of the night. They hear sounds. They're
locked in tight, all right, but they hear someone fooling at

the door and windows. 'Go away!' they say. 'Who is it?' There is silence, and then a voice says, 'We are thieves, let us in.' That somehow is so typical. I don't think they are really cruel. Wait." She edged forward, signaling Tess to say nothing. She sat back.

"Gareth is still on about crime. It's coming up a sermon—how criminal, how worthless the Batswana are. How slow they are. 'They move like clouds,' he likes to say. They are so insanitary and so forth and so on ad nauseam world without end. It wears me right out. Not that I wasn't that way. I was worse, at first. I was just a maniac when food fell on the floor and one of the children picked it up to eat, because the help are barefoot— What is it?"

Tess was pressing a palm to her middle and frowning. She put a finger to her lips and slid closer to Nan. In a low voice, she said, "I'm ovulating. I get a stitch over here when it starts. Or on the other side."

"You mean without fail? So you always know where you are?"

"All my life."

"Aren't you lucky!" Nan said. Her eyes reddened, and she turned to look out the window on her side.

They had been passing through a long stretch of burned-over land. The bleakness oppressed them. The women began estimating how far it was to Lobatse, their destination. Tom corrected them. "Ladies, you are too low by half. It's three hours from here to the pavement, with the worst driving yet to come—the deep sand near Pala, the Trench. Then on the bitumen it's an hour and a half to Lobatse, the Cumberland Hotel, a lager, fillet chasseur, a bathe, and good night all and thank you very much."

He offered the water bottle. Tess drank from it, but Nan said no. She explained to Tess, "In truth, I am parched, but

I don't want to make Gareth pull up for my comfort more than I have to—especially near Pala. There we must have momentum." Tess set the bottle on the seat next to her.

"Just look at this country," Nan said. "Red rock wilderness. It makes one sad, really."

Tess made a sympathetic face.

They began tacking. Here the road was braided around dry sinks and sharp rock outcrops. The women looked commiseration at one another. The vehicle ran close to the bank on some curves. Brush scraped the windows.

The driving eased, finally. The men were murmuring about the road mess in Botswana. They were cynical. Nan sat forward, straining to hear. Contractors were using shoddy materials. Service trenches were subsiding through lack of proper compaction. Heavy equipment was being dragged across fresh tarmac without rollers. There were too few bell-mouths.

Nan interrupted. "Do I understand you to be saying that all the trouble with the new roads is *not* just the Botswana government people but, aha!, bad workmanship by outsiders—whites, isn't it?—from South Africa and from Europe?"

"Well, to an extent, yes," Gareth said.

"Well, if you know about this, why don't you inform government? I'm sure they'd be grateful."

"They don't want to hear it."

"Oh, do they not? How do you know? Have you tried?"

"One can't just go and point a finger. They don't want to hear this. We are not road engineers, are we now?"

"No, but you are *engineers*. Mine engineers, but you know something about materials, and you seem to know quite a lot about roads, too, as it seems. So why not tell government?"

Tom said, "Waste of breath. You may believe that. You listen to your husband."

"They don't want to hear it," Gareth said again, more firmly.

"But then a letter. Anonymous. Or write the *Daily News*. They print letters."

Both men laughed, then said, "Not likely," in unison, which made them laugh again.

Nan raised her voice. "Why don't you go to, oh, *anyone*, then? Go to the High Commission instead of just sitting there laughing at the sheer folly of ever, ever, ever trying seriously to help these poor wretches get something they pay for! You won't even try! Because even if there are pirates you won't do it. Tess, this is what I am ill with. Just this."

Gareth spoke in an even, ominous tone. "You are exciting yourself. We'll not have it. There is nasty driving coming and you are doing this. Tess, can you assist? We are not alone in this vehicle, Nan."

"Oh, you don't like what I say—what a surprise! You don't care for the people here, and there is an end of it. The smallest thing I propose is always senseless, madness—I must put it from me. Like the tins the workmen boil up their mealie pap in for breakfast and tea, No. 10 size. They are just boiling the lead from the seams straight into their food. Now, it *cannot* be sound. I spoke to the sisters, and they said, 'Good heavens, are they?' Tess, not even will he get a proper three-leg pot or two for his own men. That would *interfere*."

"You are making a row!" Gareth shouted.

Nan said, still loud, "Yes. Talking of rows, Tess, listen. Last week, blazing rage. For what? First, you know all the beef this country sends abroad. All right, they don't eat much beef. Certainly the poor hardly see it unless the chief has something to celebrate. No, the beef is kept to multiply, and then, when they need cash, it goes straight to the abattoir and then straightaway into tins and to Europe—England. Because grass-fed beef makes up perfectly into baby food, Tess. Now, what drove him to rage was this mad idea of mine: Why can't government just save aside some portion of the tinned baby food and provide it to mothers free through clinics—why not?"

Gareth broke in. "I'll tell you why, because the mothers would eat it, wouldn't they?"

"Oh, Gareth! You shame me! Yes, all right. Some would. But a lot would get to the babies. The mothers are hungry, too. And the babies go straight from the breast to mealie pap, starch. And it kills a lot of them—indirectly—Tess."

"Mealie has protein," Gareth said.

"Ah, but so little! And one can just look at the size of the people. The men are small. Answer me why the meat must go only to the fair babies of Europe."

"You know my answer."

"Well, state it for Tess and Tom, or just for Tess, then—by now they are fascinated."

"It is not our part! That would be the dole, and the government are dead set they will not have that, and quite right. Now enough!"

"And that's all you truly see?"

"All there is, isn't it? Ah." They had reached the last high point before the Pala stretch. The men were relieved.

"The Trench!" Tom said. "There it is."

Tess said softly to Nan, "We must be still."

Very softly, Nan said, "You know I don't hate him, Tess, do you?"

Tess patted Nan's shoulder.

The last of the sun was in their eyes as they descended. Gareth came down into the deep sand with good speed. The long ascent began well. The trick was to stay precisely in the spoors cut by the last vehicle preceding. There were hazards to avoid, the worst being the loose meshes of brush, like nests, which had earlier been packed into soft places in the track by drivers who had gotten stuck. Gareth scanned the road far ahead. There was right-of-way for only one vehicle. If two vehicles met, one would have to climb up into the side drifts or reverse to the last spot wide enough to permit clearance. Gareth was taut.

The road was below the level of the land. The banks at this point ran even with their shoulders. Nan looked to the rear. The dust plume they were churning up extended as far back as she could see—solid, like a wall. For some time, no one spoke.

They saw something in the middle distance ahead—a figure, and then figures, on the right bank, motioning. Grim, Gareth said, *"Na lifti."*

Nan said, "Nobody is saying give lifts, Gareth. We are quite presentably full up. No fear."

The figures grew closer.

"It's *bushies!*" Tom said.

"No, it's too far south—can't be," Gareth said.

"No, it is, it is—it's bushies," Tom said. "They must be clear over from the pan. It must be the drought. I hear the pan is dried up. God, that is a distance to come. Dear God above. It is. There's a string of them. Want us to stop."

"Well, good luck," Gareth said.

"Bushmen—Basarwa," Nan said. "But only women."

"Hard to tell," Tom said, trying to be light.

Tess said, "Oh, pity—they must want to trade ostrich shells or that beadwork. They want tobacco or salt or anything. Sugar. Too bad. They just give it away if you have what they want. Oh, too bad. I have some lovely things. Oh, pity we can't stop and see. Well, that is life."

The banks were lower here. They drew even with the

Basarwa—two young girls and an older woman with an infant caught against her front in a leather sling, all gesturing urgently.

Tess said, "They look so Chinese—they are all cheekbones; look at it."

The women were close to the road. Two of them were holding out pots or cans. The girls were waving the vessels up and down, stiffly, frantically. The mother dropped into an odd posture, like kneeling prayer, but clapping her hands under her chin. They made a tableau. The Rover approached. The women were dressed in skins and rags. They were thin. Nan stared. Arms and legs were like sticks. Their hair seemed to grow in dots on their skulls. One girl appeared to be wearing a kind of cap, but it was a huge scab, Nan saw. All were smiling unnaturally at the vehicle as it passed slowly. They were calling out. Nan opened her window. It was impossible to understand anything.

"Will you *slow*, Gareth?" Nan asked. "I can't hear them."

Gareth said nothing.

The faces did look Oriental, except for the hair. The mother got up. The whole group began to trot alongside.

Nan opened the window fully and put her head out. Tess pulled at her.

"Can we not slow, Gareth?" Nan asked urgently.

"They're trading," Gareth answered.

"No," Nan said. "They're saying '*metse*.' That's it. We must stop, Gare. I have it clear."

Tess said, "What on earth is *metse*? *I* don't have any."

"*Water*, Tess. They want water. I have never heard of this. They don't do this. Look, they're keeping up. This is too desperate. We must stop. We have the outer tank. It's full of water. We must stop. Gare, I am pleading! I am faint. You must stop. Stop this. We have the external tank. You must *attend*. They are all running. One of the girls, Gare—a scab condition. They are smiling at us, begging. Gare, if you love me, *please stop!*"

"They can run for miles, they say," Tess said.

"That is the men, Tess—when they *hunt*."

"Right. They blow poison darts, and that weakens the animal or rhino or what all, and then they just·run after it until it drops. Days, sometimes, it takes. They can run."

"Tess, be still. Look at them."

The Basarwa were reaching to touch or catch hold of the vehicle.

"Gare," Nan said. "What do you say? Please, my heart, we *must* stop!" She put her hands on his shoulders. He tensed and bucked violently to reject her touch.

Gareth said, "There is no chance. We are in sand, Nan. We could be all night. *No!*" He was increasing speed.

"Then, Gare," she said, "if we stick, all right, we could put brush down—I would help. I would help. Please, Gare. The mother is running. Their mother is running. We won't stick. Help can turn up. They are skin and bone!" She appealed to Tess. "They are skin and bone. We are making them run."

Again Nan put her head out the window. The Land-Rover was drawing away. Nan could hear the dire breathing of the runners.

"No stopping, I say," Tom said.

Nan ducked back in. "Tom, this is our vehicle!" she said, shouting.

"You shall be civil to Tom," Gareth said, in his most menacing voice.

Nan saw one of the girls drop to the ground, spent.

"One of the girls has fallen."

"Nan, we are picking up dust. You will close up. Close the window."

Gareth was right. There was dust in the air. "Hear,

hear!" Tess said. She had taken out a bandanna and was holding it bunched near her mouth.

Nan closed the window and sat back, making herself look forward, her face agonized.

"They are still at the side, Gareth," Nan said. "Gare, at the window you can see them, two of them. Gare, please look. Oh, *help!*"

Nan opened the window again. She looked back. The second girl had fallen. Only the mother, still carrying the baby, was still pursuing, her face wild. She would soon fall.

"The mother is still running, Gareth. She is straining, with that baby. I wish you would look. You are destroying me. *We must stop!*"

The mother was heaving with effort. It was too much. She threw her arms up and fell on her back, protecting the infant she was carrying.

The Land-Rover ground onward. Nan looked to the rear. The women were lost. She covered her face with her hands. Then she lowered her hands and seized the water bottle from Tess, who was holding it. She shoved her window open and hurled the bottle out onto the bank. She lunged toward the front, grasping for anything else she could find to throw out of the vehicle. The men shouted. Tom grappled with her. Tess shrank into her corner. Tom turned and got on his knees in his seat and seized Nan by the shoulders. He pressed her back. He held her. Gareth was trembling with fury.

"She has pitched out the water bottle, Gareth," Tom said.

With a roaring cry that frightened them all, Gareth drove his foot down on the brake. The Rover slewed and stopped. The engine died. Tom released Nan.

They sat in silence, tilted, mastering themselves. Nan was the first to speak. "Why have we stopped, Gareth?" she whispered.

Gareth was contained. "One of us must collect the bottle. Simple enough."

For a moment they were in darkness, enclosed in the dust of their passage as the wind came up sharply behind them. Nothing could be done until it was clear again. They waited.

Tom moved to get out. But Gareth caught Tom's wrist and pulled him roughly back. "One of us must collect the bottle," Gareth said again.

THIEVING

As from 1978, God chose me for a thief. Could I, a boy, withstand Him? If God marks you, you must fall, always.

Why must God choose out one Mokgalagadi who is poor and who in all times past loved all things of God and B.V.M.? I was very much in churches. I was foremost in singing of hymns, praising God most highly. My name of Paul is found in Scripture. To me, God hates all thieves. And if Lord Jesus may forgive a thief at times, always it is just because this thief is vowing he shall steal no more. What book is my greatest treasure, if not *St. Joseph Daily Missal*?

As well, I am Mokgalagadi, of a tribe that in all ages of time is misfortunate and despised in Botswana and always made to be enslaved and mocked, and having any treasures taken from it, never taking them from others. Only Basarwa are less than we to the prideful Bamangwato and Bakwena, our masters. At Tsane I never took items from my mother as children do. Always I was truthful. I only sought to prosper with good English-speaking. My tutor was Sister Honoria at St. Boniface Mission, godsent to me. But she was taken out from Tsane to aid others.

I came to my fate by an egg, at Lobatse, at Boiteko School. A cooked egg came to be found in my bed. At Boiteko, we few Bakgalagadi were ill treated by Bamalete and Coloured boys at times, myself the most. It was because I am tall, and fast in my English. I was first in Geography by far. To this day I state Headmaster Sebina and the bursar Chibaya made a crime ring, with hiding of sports fees and claiming of a cashbox stolen, with, then, Sebina found as owner of a new van for hire. They feared inspectors coming. So that if some boys could be shown out as thieves for taking food and cooked eggs from the kitchen, those boys could be given all blame, and so forward with more crimes! They said Here is Paul Ojang who is late on fees and with no relations to aid him in the Board of Trust, and he is a boarder from far-distant Tsane, from where he cannot be heard again. So a miracle passed and an egg was found to walk. Still today I can cry at this wrong done to me.

The cur Sebina said I was only telling falsehoods—he, the master liar. When that cashbox was taken, keen boys were sleeping two hands from the office, yet they heard no sounds when doors were broken through. Miracles were all about. I said to him If at all I am a thief, why am I known to say to some chaps who are stealing in shops in Lobatse it is wrong? But he said I must pack and go. He said I was known to name him as Headmonster. He knew it only from spies. Who set that egg into my bed? It was boys or the crime ring, or God's hand.

At any time, Sebina stopped our food, as when there was a turmoil at film night. Always he would punish us a day when there must be meat provided. He sold our meat, I know it. Always the head boy for our form was in fear, because I said he must report to the inspectors on all manner of wrong-doing. I said he must report as to food, as to cabbages crushing us day upon day. But he was afraid.

Why was I not given strokes only, if I took that egg? It was because I had no protector. My father is unknown. My form mates were silent. Sebina forced me to sit one night through at Central Transport yard, with my goods, to wait for the Bedford sent to carry me in shame back to Tsane. I was chopped from my Junior Certificate by that cur with yellow eyes.

You are put to shame. You must go atop a Bedford to your mother, who shall thrash you. You must hold fast to ropes. Your goods are pushed under ropes. Much wind scrapes off tears from your cheeks. When you need some water, there is just but one hosepipe siphon, used the same for petrol and for taking water, so you must fall ill with swallowed petrol. You shall be sent to herding by your mother. After Kanye you come to bush, with no houses. At Jwaneng Mine, you pass far-distant houses behind fences caused by diamonds buried there. After Jwaneng it is bush evermore. Those drivers were fast.

What! at Sekgoma Pan those drivers turned from the road to go straight for the bush. They shall make me a mother too soon, was said by Monusi Maome, a pregnant girl who was a passenger with me. They were shaking us every way. At last they halted at a tree. They jumped down with rifles to go for duiker, whilst sparing no words to us of returning back.

What must I find at Tsane? Thrashings, a mother ever seeking beer, harsh words and all such things until I am forced away to Ghanzi to work for Boers. Of all whitemen, you cannot love them, even if as brother citizens we should do. You cannot love these white Batswana, in no way. Because they will not teach you. In the freehold farms you are paid by food and with some pinches of coins at times. You toil endless days.

I determined I must go before those men returned back, go to the capital even if I must go every click by foot. Then I took down my goods and took from them what I could carry, and all the rest put under heaped-up stones, laughing because it was a beacon for thieves to come, I knew it. I took clothes, provisions, water, my best books: *St. Joseph Missal* and my set-book of *Shane*. I took farewell of Monusi, who was saying I must stay with her. She said I must post a letter to my mother, from Gaborone, at the soonest. She said to guard as to snakes. I went away, marching, trusting to God to help a boy.

I fled fast from Sekgoma Pan, lest those men come searching. As well, the closer you become to Jwaneng, you are the safer as to lions, which do not venture nearby Jwaneng unless at drought times. I was bold, striving with all things such as hunger and hot sun. I made two lifts, always by Europeans. One night I lay in a tree. I lay all one day in the gum-tree forest at Lobatse, too weak. I was quenched out.

I came to our capital. I saw rich housing, tarred streets, vehicles crowding up. Yet every day my schemes were blasted. In all shops a sign says *Ga Gona Tiro:* No Work in Here. With no sponsor, no testimonial, no relations, I saw I must become as animals. By night I lay in the bush nearby the university, changing my place at times. I must wash up in Bontleng at some standpipes. By day I asked jobs or sought to carry parcels at the Hyper Store amongst the *tsotsi* boys, forcing myself foremost among them. All about Gaborone you discern many boys with no home. My funds were drained. I dreamed of milk.

A cobbler sits amidst a multitude of shoes, at Dove Close. I said I can be apprentice to you. He felt my hands and saw I was a student. He said no. I said But I can carry shoes to homes roundabouts for payment, because now you must wait endless days for payment. But he asked if at all I would give gold coins for polishing to a vagabond. I went away. They no more take novices for the mines in South Africa. I went for labor at the Industrial Site, for building work, but was thrust back by ruffians. Biting sores came in the sides of my mouth. I feared always as to lice.

Ever slowly I was sinking down, until God moved his hand to give me aid, a savior, the true thief Elias Odireng.

He was called Alias. He found me in a ruin, lying ill. That ruin was to be a bottle store one day. But in those times it was mere walls. Work was stopped, it seems. No watchman came. Bush was springing back from whence it had been chopped. He was three years my senior. Already he had been at prison. He knew this place where I was found. He knew many sites. At once he took pity. He said if I am well I can aid him many ways. If he would bring some girls there, I could stand lookout. He prophesied I would soon be healed by him.

So at once he was gone to steal food. He made true feasts, with pilchards, sour milk, scones, polonies, tinned sea fish, Pine Nut soda and others, Fray Bentos tinned beef, *naartjies*, some cooked foods still warmed, peaches, mince, sweets. All thanks to him I was made well.

I said Where can you unearth such food? He said he would gladly tell me just because he would soon be gone to South Africa, to Diepkloof, to join in thieving cars with guys he knew from prison, soon to be free. He was awaiting one master-thief only. He said on Notwane Road I should find two houses wherein Peace Corps guys were passing through. He said that if at all they hide door keys it is in one place only. He said they were carefree, most times not locking that place whatever. I must take plastic sakkies in my pocket and go to the kitchen, but I must take only sums of food, never the whole of any food. But I must never take beers, because then Peace Corps guys would go raging all about, with lights switched on, eager for fighting. He said You can rob there every day, with ease. Too many guys are holding food in just one fridge, he said. I said Why do they not complain to the police. He said Because they are themselves thieves, and you shall see very many plates and tumblers marked from Rhodesian Railways in those hostels.

Always sometimes now I say what! was this thief a Holy Guardian Angel and not a true man, not born out of a woman, in fact? Because it says in *St. Joseph* at page 1078 that everyone of the faithful has a Guardian Angel from God, even unto some pagans as well. I know this page until today. On it the Lord God says *I am sending my Angel to guard you and bring you to the place I have prepared.* Alias was very quick in coming and going, like a ghost. He was ever advising against evils such as cigarettes and beer drinking. And as well he healed me in so short a time and prophesied when I should be made well and going about. What was he? He ate in small amounts. The house dogs thereabout were silent when he was there. He was very becoming, he was smooth-faced, with no initiation scars. At every hour he advised me. He said I must never borrow someone any money. He said You must not hide stolen things at your mother's house, for the police always go first to her. He warned against long-holding of stolen goods, saying you must sell them, even for a little, to escape danger. He showed me to make tea in a jar of water set in sunlight, with no fire. Amounts of good things fell from this known thief, to confuse me.

Soon one morning he was gone. Withinside my shoe was twenty pula, left by him. I was cast down. Never shall I see his face again.

I was once more at Hyper Store, amongst those boys. They said Chumza, hello, where is your boyfriend Alias, tell us for we must see him, where is that guy just now? I said to them he was gone. Now they said What! he has taken so much cash and some items from us, promising studies with a mastermind thief from Diepkloof. I said On this I know nothing. They told to me all that he was promising: means against watchdogs, means for temptation of servants, means to divine if someone is abroad within a dark house, much about keys, much about thieving through window bars with wire hooks. They pushed me, and after many kind of threats said they shall watch me day unto night. They said to beware them.

Those were cruel days, I may say. Always I wished only to slip down from God's eye. I ceased from prayers. I ceased from reading of *St. Joseph*. At the library I could not be granted pockets, as I had no postal bag, so I must study books there what hours I could steal from bearing parcels, weary and too weak. I feared as to my English, with no studies and conversing.

At last one night I saw great throngs passing in at Town Council Hall, rejoicing. It was when after long struggle Zimbabwe was free in victory. Some way I could not be glad in this, because in this free nation of Botswana I was not progressing. Soon those bush fighters would be as kings in Zimbabwe, and it was said many brave fighters were in fact mere boys, not school-trained even up to Standard Three.

In no way could I gain a seat within. Thick as bees, some guys made noises chatting even whilst ministers were giving off statements of great importance. Therefore I lingered on the outside, regarding many posters of the war that were stating as to all kind of tasks and vowing *chimurenga* many times over.

So at once a fat whiteman saw me there. He was rushing, with a camera. He said to come aside to the shadows. With no greetings whatsoever he asked me if I speak English and if I can greatly help him. If I can swiftly pull down some posters, he shall give me at his house three pula each, which he said as "puler." He said he must go forward to the stage, else he should pull down these mementos for himself. He stayed in Seepapitso Crescent, plot number three-zed-twenty. He said I am a friend to these comrades, never fear.

Those posters are mounted up with mere spots of chewing gum, he said. Others shall take them, he said, unless we are fast.

All whilst he spoke, I said to beware, for this was thieving. But yet if this guy was well pleased, I could venture with asking any kind of job from him. So I saw I must do it.

In all I saved six posters, very fast. Then at once some guys saw me, hailing out cries that said I was a traitor. So I ran fast, going all about amongst vehicles until I could turn up these things tight into a stick and thus escape.

All the night to come I was fearful. As children we are made always to beseech God. But I was blocked from prayer, fearing even as to prayers to Sister Honoria, a mortal, because clergy are at all times watched on by God. But at last I saw my hope. I said if you hand up these things freely for no payments whatsoever, you are no thief, and this guy will be the more pleased about it. If at all there was to be a thief, he would be the thief, as I would take nothing. So at that I slept on.

I found his place with ease, as there was a sign naming Jarvis and the plot number as I had it. My heart played fast, for all this plot within the fence was in ruins and untidy. Dog holes stood throughout the street fence. I said what! a Type One house with no one raking, arms of trees scraping on the roof, gum-tree bark fallen down, dry gardens. It was evening-time.

There was no dog about, yet signs stated to beware a dog. I walked slowly there. I saw dark ghostly quarters at the rear, thus there were no servants with them, I was sure of it. His Land-Rover was brown with dust all over. I was at the back way. A white woman was before me in the kitchen. In her lips a Santos Dumont burned whilst she cooked up meat, stirring. I knocked the windowpane. She too was fat. She shook her head, sharp, as if to send me straight away, and thus some ashes of her smoking fell down into that food. She took no notice, I may say. I have no job, she said. *Ga ke na tiro*, she said, over again.

So I went at the front to find this man. He was there. I knocked. He rejoiced at once, with those posters in his hands. He said I must come in. He said we must see them, both together. That floor was in disorder. We pushed articles aside. That place was heaped on every hand with books, journals, all kind of papers and photographs widespread, tumblers, photographs in boxes. He praised those posters endlessly. He must have his wife to see. That place was in great disorder.

Soon enough it came up to payments. I refused. Then he said he cannot believe me. At once I spoke of work. I said I can do yard work. I said I was homeless. Still always I refused money. He said they must forever have no servants, because of some very great beliefs. I told him of my straits. He said I must take more money than three pula for each one. But always still I refused. Then he said I must take tea.

He went aside to his wife to discuss. He said they can hire me. It was against her will, I could hear it, and worst as it came up to accommodation. She was in fear lest she always overtake me on the inside of her house. He said there was Primus and WC in quarters, so I can stay out. As well, he said if I should go there they can cease their shame as to many Batswana homeless and no one in that empty place. But she said she was afraid lest I arouse her every day from sleep as I set about working. He said But sometimes if I am away a gecko can drop down upon you, as we know, and this lad can chase it out. But she said Why must you forever force this thing when our food is hot?—that is the only reason you are succeeding. So at the end it was all right, but I must swear to many rules. I must never use such words as master or mistress, and many other rules as well.

So at last I was a bit safe. I could lock my goods. Mma Jarvis gave to me all such things as chairs, wardrobe, table, pots, cloths, tub, Primus cooker, bed, paraffin lamp, as well as mealie, thousand cabbages, and wash-powder. Can you borrow me some books at times? I said to Rra Jarvis. You may choose every book, he said. With all pleasure he would do it. Very great-sized atlas, he borrowed me at once, and more books thereafter. Really, those people were by far too carefree, with payments time and again beyond my terms. He said I must become more fat. He explained me *chimurenga* as "great storm of people," very freely, so I said there can be many countless questions solved at last.

Endless days I worked to clean that plot and all the verge as well. I healed some trees, I know it. I scalded ants within their holes. I pulled down mistletoe from trees. Where termites pushed their nest mud high on tree sides, I scraped them to hell. I was a savior many fold. Guys passing in the road saw me watchful there and stepped onwards. Because you can go for asking jobs and just take some things. You can open cars. You can take shirts found hanging.

That man was strong for Africans, I may say. Without fail at morning he would shower curses on the news reader of Springbok station from Johannesburg, as You are murderers, or cretins, at times. Refugee guys came there rather much for drinks and meals. He was helping them.

By my terms of work, I must be always without the house. Mma Jarvis was ever painting scenes of life and must be in silence thus. So it was okay. I liked it best. I was progressing. Soon I would post a letter to my mother, I knew.

But all too soon, what! I must be made to have a house key. They must go some days to Tuli Block on holiday. I said I rathermore have no key, yet they said I must. They praised me. I must only switch on lights at night, and water in some

pots of plants. My heart was choked. If at all some goods or
cameras could go missing, they would name one thief: Paul
Ojang. Thrice I spoke against this. But I was forced to hold
a key, in fact. Before I took that house key, Mma Jarvis gave
me oftentimes the key for post, that I must bring. All such
signs of trust were scaring to me.

At my tasks withinside, I ran, to finish off and be spared.
I said I must cope up. That house was pushed full. You dis-
cerned such things heaped, as, fish traps, beer sieves, thousand baskets, thumb harps, Basarwa aprons and pouches,
some spears, stools, cameras, wood serpents and *tokoloshi,*
books just tossed. I looked straight to my task.

So but when they returned back from Tuli Block and all
was well, they said I must hold that key for all time. But
when thrice I refused, he agreed to say okay. He said he
likes me. He wished greatly he could one day arising find
all government officers gone at one blow and fine boys in
their place, rather. He said You shall be perm sec one day,
I know it.

I was prospering, if I may say. Because he said I can
make a market garden if it pleases me. So every day I was
selling freely amongst cookmaids such things as marrows,
tamaties, radish, and lettuces. As well, he vowed he will
never surcharge me as to water. I was rich, a bit. He gave
me seeds he had from others.

Soon one day he said I must aid in *omnium gatherum,*
great function for honoring some heroes. These too were
refugees, but heroes set free from prison in South Africa. I
must stand close and listen to such guys passing through
Botswana. He praised those guys the most by far. First I
must dig a *braai*-pit and clean about the plot as if Jesus will
be at tea, he said. He must hire lights in all colors.

But at that function I served out goat meat and *wors*
countless hours, longing to be freed. At last I could go. But
then I must make errands for the woman, to find some costly

steel-made platters demanded by the caterers and lost. When I came to eat, it was at best bread rolls and beetroot salad, and some guava seeds left in fluids. Turmoil! Over-drinking on beer and Autumn Harvest! That place was thronged full. I saw many guys from university, two perm secs, Europeans, refugees, Angolans, two Chinese men, Swazis. I went to hear at last.

It was hot, with motor fans switched on. It was too full in that parlor. On the outside, guys pressed to our flyscreens, in time commanding anyone to switch off some fans to help them hear Sinuka well enough. It was half-twelve.

All those South Africans stood as one, nearby the hero Sinuka, guarding and watchful always. Great unceasing arguments! Those guys were sharp, finding out very many falsehoods spoken there. I liked them.

Now at once Sinuka was repeating on one theme. He said In Azania, when the Boers are overthrown, we the Africans shall take all power over shops and mines of all kind, as to banks, as to farms, no matter if some Europeans or UK have put their money in keeping of the Boers at one time. At this, some Europeans hopped up. One said All that is mere thieving, then, and you shall forge enemies out of once-true friends, if you do so. Sinuka cried out some way.

Then I was blasted once again, because Sinuka said Yes, we shall be thieves, because you Europeans have taken Africa and all that is upon it from us over many years' time, and we have studied you well and shall become as you, who are the greatest thieves under God's eyes! He said Yes, you must call us thieves, for we are graduands of long years' teaching and must be proud! He said If you steal from a thief who has tutored you, are you then a thief at all, for if you say yes, then very well! Thieves forward!

Here was danger calling me. I said I shall never follow thieves. So I went away, rather trembling.

I passed some days in fear. I said to be brave.

Soon enough God slashed me twice. I make it three days from that function. A cookmaid of the Vice Mayor came, stating I must tell you from the radio that your mother is late! What! I said, you cannot tell me so! She said It is from that program of messages of such things, they are searching out Paul Ojang. Your mother was taken by sickness, at Tsane, she said. I was crying, then, for my late mother and for being left alone as such.

Mothers, never be rash! Because one day we must recall you. And ever be watchful as to funds! I journeyed by costly transport to Tsane. At Tsane I met charges on every hand. Our herd was long sold up, I knew, yet some men told me of two beasts taken as strays, yet she always failed to claim them at the chief's kraal, so they fell to him in time. She was a defaulter at the health post. I was left with medicines and rubbish. From on the hill, I saw beasts going every way upon Tsane Pan to find out water, like ants. The pan was cracked. Sand wind came over day by day. Many houses there stand empty.

I feared about my saved money at Tsane and my fear was proved. I wished only to return back from there. A pastor asked money more and more, as to burial charges. Even if a mother is a scourge to you, you must regret when she is late, it seems. I was too sad there. I must soon return to my smooth-walled housing at Seepapitso Crescent or become mad. I feared as to my lettuces.

It was at Kanye I said may that egg be my clue to riches. I said Jarvis must let me to rear up chickens to be sold. They take little water, as they bathe in dust. I saw I could gain back some funds quite fast.

Then, I was returned back. No matter if it was on Sunday, I set to work. But in days, what! God moved his waiting blow.

Jarvis called me to come to them for sweets. Then it was told to me. I must leave them, as they must quit our nation to stay untold years in Mozambique. I fell sick at heart. I cried. It was to make a film about Frelimo and how that struggle could win out. He must go for duty. He was summoned to it. Once more I was chopped from hope, just crying, as God pleased.

Where could I turn? At night I was even retching. By one fortnight I must aid Stuttafords to pack up their goods completely and be left alone. Was I not like Shane, who only wished to be a farmer yet was forced once again to fire upon his fellowmen? Or was I not as some saints, because many saints were forced, as to marrying of pagans, or beheading, like Felicitas, by God the ruler over all this world?

Rra Jarvis came to raise my cheer some way. He said Letty is striving, ringing up some women every day to unearth a post with accommodation. For farewell, he gave me a dictionary of words.

At last a job was found out. They said I may go as yard boy for some people differing to Jarvises but yet nice. Mma said All what you do for us is just all right to us if it is your true best, but these Wrens are rich to an extent. Thus you must work to perfection, she said. I should have coveralls provided and accommodation up to a sleeping-room, but no shower-place or toilet to myself, of course. She said This Rra Wren is high director of your nation's bank and shall stay this side some five years until returning back to London, so you can be full grown. She said As well, he can sponsor you for Capital Continuation night studies if he likes you well enough, but I am not too sure.

She advised me all kind of things, over again. Never must I purge my nostrils in my fingers. Always I must guard on bearing tales. One thing above others she said many times: I must befriend that woman, because she was very

strained with bad fortune. If at all Batswana might tease or
so, they were only misled. She was nice, Mma Jarvis said.
She was American. Mma Jarvis bought me varied new clothing, with shoes. She said I was bonny. Every day she gave
me presents such as half-remaining foods as chutney, sun-
flower oil, *tamatie sous*, maizena, bread crumbs in packets,
some tins of lichees, jelly, dry soup.

Rra Jarvis brought me there. That place was risen from the
dreaming brains of a thief. All about was wealth. You must
enter by two gates in order. You must give in your name and
reasons. You can see one man with no duties beyond tending
on dogs. Another is hunting over and forth along the walks
to pinch out any spear of grass to come amongst the pave-
ments. You pass hedges made as balls and boxes throughout,
many lawns, many bowers growing. You see Waygards always two and two, so that if one should chance to sleep, his
comrade shall report on him. Everything in that place, you
must crave for. The air itself must be made sweet, by women
with spray-canisters, at times.

At once Bastiaan brought me to sit withinside. He commanded tea. Bastiaan was headservant there, or captain, a
Xhosa, very fierce, to me. He was like Ken Gampu. His
head was shaved. He wore fine suits. He took away my letter
of reference, leaving me. Those carpets were soft, to make
you wish to spring about. My plate was gold-ringed. My
serviette was in a bracelet.

I saw this master was one for fish and the sea. All on the
walls were caught fish, as thick-through as dogs, made hard
and shining. Save for pilchards, we Batswana do not trust in
fish. Far in the north, the Mmukushu are fish-eating, but we
do not know them well and they are from Angola, really.

At once I was brought farther, to Mma Wren. It was by
day, yet she wore dark glasses. She was white-haired and

white-dressed. She discussed with Bastiaan about my letter, a time, discerning me through those dark glasses. She said Are you quiet? Because here we are quiet. It was true, because that staff was quiet-spoken, differing to the shouting and ragging staffs of houses roundabout Jarvises. She said she regretted as to my mother. She pressed my hands. She wore gold finger rings and gold hair clips. She was little. Then it was fixed. I may come and toil amongst all those treasures.

Those maids were as cruel as nurses. I alone of all Batswana in that place refused to laugh against Mma Wren in secret. They would speak insults of her in Setswana at any time, if only Bastiaan was not nearby, of course. They said I must think what fanciful meaning I can say for my surname when she shall ask me. They said she was well-pleased when Bibiana Matlhapeng told that her name meant "There are too many rocks in this place," and as well when Kebonyetsala Gaolekwe told that her surname says "You cannot do anything to God." But I said those were true meanings. They said You are just argumental. They said You must be fanciful and please her, she is like a child. They said Others have done so. They said She is ever saying we Batswana are too mean at times with naming our children, as when Bibiana named her son Molebi, "He who is ever staring at you." They said She says it is not fair on children and she bothers us on this, extremely. As well, they said Mma Wren is ever asking why certain kind of English first-names are given, as, Extra, or Fabric. They said She must not tell Tswana people how to put names, yet she does so. They said But we name our children as we please, and we give names as Beauty or Idol, if we please, so this white woman must just cease. They said she torments them. They said You shall see, she shall carry you *Daily News* asking why is this man named as Icks, or Slow, or Lucifer.

In those days Mma Wren must no longer drive freely on her own, but only go about with Bastiaan or Rra Wren. It was because when once she was driving, she stopped in North Ring Road but not pulling to one side, these women said, because she wished to chase up an albino boy. They said Mma Wren stated that this boy was over-red from sunlight and that albinos could die thus, they must all wear broad hats in summertime. Those women said She is mental, that is all, she is mental. They said Now she is held from driving, as she made commotions in North Ring. She is bewitched, they said, she has transgressed something, so she has become mental, and it is we alone who must suffer. And they said The master bought that Peugeot for a present for her alone, at one time. She fears fires, they said.

At Wrens we were Tswana in our food: mealie and sorghum. We must join to stamp mealie. Those women would beg and tease to make me join. Food from the table was sent for the dogs, and these women saw it, bemoaning. But worse by far was about the fruits, because Mma Wren must have filled-full baskets in every room, of apples and bananas growing spots, and these fruits were just lost. But I said this rule was good, in fact, because those women would scheme about who is to get this or so, as to who would be favored. We were too many. As to stamping, in secret I liked it because at each stroke I fancied I am stamping down God and his snares, to become safe. When the drought came, you could not buy costly fruit, so these women raged the more. But they watched against Bastiaan, who can hear as far as birds.

Rra Wren's many books were fit for a thief, with gold letters and all such things. You cannot ask to loan such books, I knew. So I was silent. For speaking English, those maids refused me every way. They said I was tormenting them. Some Batswana tell you everything of English is just torment and that some day it shall be thrown down. At school, if you should speak Setswana in the hearing of teachers, it was told to you it would bring strokes. But that was false. Many Batswana teachers spoke Setswana in classes, with no shame. The cur Sebina told that head boys must report on Setswana-speaking at play-times or revision, but never did they. I was brave many times to say back words in English for Setswana said by older boys, but they came to hate me and said I was a traitor and scheming Mokgalagadi.

I was caring for that rose bower above all. After midday it was allowed for staff to sleep, but I alone would not sleep on many days, but would at times be found reading in *St. Joseph*. Now, Mma Wren could as well be found in that bower, under the net-shade, with some drinks. Those maids ragged me for not sleeping as they did. Ever slowly, Mma Wren grew kind to me. She asked my name over again. She said I must sit in a chair, not upon the ground, for reading. Those maids said Why must you go that side to read?—you can read here, we have chairs if you greatly love to sit in a chair, you can do so among us. Of course, Batswana must ever love best to lie or sit at ease upon the earth, as we know. They said I was seeking favor. That was their way, always, yet all were strong Christians. Mma Wren saw I was one for books. So she said can I be most careful if she finds some precious books for me to read? She said I must never harm or mislay them, only. I said yes. Always she repeated how precious were these books to come. She would give me one at one time and I must return it back to her perfect as she gave it to me. She said these were the most precious books to a boy, she knew it. Over again I said I would be glad.

She came forth with one book. It was *Erik Noble and the Forty-Niners the Big Little Book*. It was old, from 1934, with pages breaking. It was one picture-page, one writing-page, all repeating up to the end. Many pages were spoiled with handwriting of a name, Brian. I read that book, sweating strings lest I break some page of it. It is about the orphan boy Erik Noble. After many countless adventures and missteps, he becomes a partner of a kind man. They make a café in San Francisco, California, at the end. I must always remember those last words, *With a young Yankee watching the cash, their enterprise had to succeed.* I handed back that book unharmed. She said I must relate how I liked that book. I said In America there is very much helping of lone boys if only they are bold and glad to work their hardest, but if it is so today I am not sure. She said she knew all boys loved these *Big Littles* and she must search to find yet more, for she had another at present time lost.

Bastiaan came to me. He said Your duties are altered, we shall say you are to work inside for training to become a steward, but it is untrue because you are too young. But Mma Wren wished me at her orders, it seems. He said she was greatly favoring me in this. Above all else, I must never put my hand to cleaning, for there would be cries unending from the house staff, but I must always say I am steward-in-training, full stop. He said Perhaps there shall be some assisting Mma Wren in cutting out of pictures from journals. But there was one room, called the sewing room, where I must pitch up every day and see what was to be. At other times she would see to my English, with lessons. Bastiaan was crossed, I saw. He said I was to be under him alone, and the mistress and master, and never under the kitchen maids, despite them. At some times I must take meals with Mma Wren, if she commanded it. He brought me to Rra Wren and left me.

It was at night. In his private room was more to do with fish, by far, with many fishing poles and chests of items. He came there to smoke. You must wish to drink down such sweet kind of smoke. He said the same to me as Bastiaan. I must help Mma Wren with filling of empty books. If she shall vanish at times to find out some thing, I must remain waiting with patience. He said one day I shall see her storeroom, which was disgracing, with many papers and mementos confused together. I must never laugh, as she was striving to bring this room to order, but too slowly. He said You can make her prosper. He said She is collecting too many damned little items from our travels world-over. As well, he said If you can, by little, question as to if she may play a bit upon the piano that is standing silent, do so. I told him my liking as to singing and indeed all kind of music. He said I was fine. Then, I must pledge to come to him, if at all I am strained or unhappy in this. Bastiaan must always stand ready to bring me straightaway to see him soonest he was at home. He said that above all things I must pitch nothing out from our endeavors, lest at some time she discern a need of it and be cast down if it was gone. Then he praised my English-speaking as a pleasure.

Those maids said I was no more than a toy of late. I made no reply. Mma Wren must keep her eyeglasses enchained about her neck and fix her watch to her breast with pins and as well with a chain for safety, and now she must have a follower at every step. In part, it was true. Mma Wren was forever searching up mislaid things with my help. Nothing was safe from her mislayings. Soon she stated I may search up items in her storeroom and bedroom, at her order. I was uneasy and in straits, because it seemed God was trying me anew, as I could freely take some thing and only say that it was lost, full stop. At that, I am a thief, full made. She said Your young eyes can find out every thing.

Most slowly we made four books full with many senseless pictures of small boys, all kind of mothers and fathers together with children. By little, I said Can we now and again bring in some pictures of musicians? She said it would be pleasing, and said Do you love music? I said What! I am great as to singing and all such things. I told how I wished to know music and instruments but was forced from school. I said You can see my voice. I sang two hymns.

Because at times I was idling there, I fell to more reasoning as to God's ways. When I set myself against thieving, always God punished me, I said. And if I go near to thieving, as with Alias and Rra Jarvis for his posters, always I am saved, I said. I saw God's doing in these endless mislayings, as a sign to me. I saw I must block this. I said perhaps if once you obey Him, He could be pleased and ask no more of you. I said if only one time God can see me a thief full-made, and see me then in straits, lamenting, He shall know His error. I said I must be as grieving mothers, or some wronged people, crying.

Rra Wren said I was fine, praising me. He said I was a jewel found. I said Many thanks. In fact, it was strange to me. If you discuss some theme, she could rise up flat and go from the room before you answer. Where did she go? To any place, to unknown rooms, about the drive, oftentimes to the garage, those maids told me. And I must just idle, or set to reading what is at hand. Still it was my best time. I drew her to the piano, by steps. Now she even played me tunes. She said You have fine hands for music. She said You shall study. I should one day read music freely, with her, she said. I saw she was my savior.

So it was then I knew I must be bold, and steal, or again be punished.

What must I take? To deceive God, it must be such as a schoolboy must covet, though I was not at school. It must be of worth and not a mere toy only. Because of danger, it must not be some prized possession of Mma Wren, lest they look straight and foremost to me as one who is at her side by far the most. It must be such as to be missed, yet not so greatly as to call forth police to oppress you. Slowly, I came to it.

It was a case out of leather. I saw it twice or so, in the garage. It was in behind some boards, pushed from view save for its handles at times. You must mount upon a box to feel it. This case was for a rich kind of student. It was old. Withinside, it held only some papers as letters and some crayon pictures from a child. It was not locked.

I took away that school case with ease, leaving no sign. I hid it for safekeeping in a hole prepared far off. I was unseen, I know it.

So I went to Bastiaan to say I must depart for two days, Saturday and Sunday, for a funeral at Mochudi. He was unkind, saying it was bad, as Rra Wren was gone to Maun for some days. But I said I am strained and I must. So he said he would allow it only for this, that he knew I would in all cases lead Mma Wren to say go. He said I must not stay off above two nights.

I went to Molepolole, not Mochudi as I told Bastiaan. Because I am too tall I can be in hotels. I stayed three nights at Slayer of Hunger Hotel—Mafenya Tlala Hotel. They said I must pay beforehand. I did. My saved money was fast going.

As to meals, I ate little, for proving to God I am oppressed even up to my hunger, even when on every hand they are eating chicken peri-peri and such things. One day I ate nothing. Over Sunday I ate mere soup and some ground-nuts, at most. I was just lingering in sorrow, waiting long hours in my chalet. I read *St. Joseph*. My scheme was to go at the last to visit Livingstone Tree that is in Molepolole. It is where Livingstone brought God and Christ upon the Batswana by his preaching. I schemed to stand nearby that tree, all sorrowing, because such a place must be at all times under God's view. When I saw that tree, what! I saw names carved freely in its side. But I saw these were names of Europeans. I said what! they have set their names down to be cursed hereafter, why? It was surprising to me. I lingered about. I said, loud, I can hang myself from this suffering, I can hang myself to this tree, even. Slowly I went away.

Yet one day farther I stayed at Molepolole, lamenting. I broke my pledge to Bastiaan. I said God must see me faced with sacking rathermore than going freely back to that place where I am now a thief. I hid from God my scheme to put that case back, in fact, as soon as I may.

Tuesday I returned back. It was late. At once I was trembling an amount, for I saw police about, and many vehicles. I was afraid. Many lights were switched on.

I said to the women What has happened? All within the house was coming and going, but no staff could be there, only Bastiaan. Bibiana said They say we are unworthy, yet at most we obeyed our mistress and now we shall be punished. Time and again I asked them to tell me what has happened.

They told me that days past Mma Wren came searching all about for some mislaid thing, but not as when a thing was mislaid in times past, because she would not say what was this thing, but only said over again to staff that they already know and must surrender it to her. Over again she refused to name this thing and thus aid them any way. She said it was precious. She accused them the more, if they said she was misled. She accused Bastiaan, in time, as well. In fact, she sacked him, commanding him to go away in his clothes. He was trying long hours to ring up Maun to find Rra Wren, with no success because those lines were down as always. She banished him off. She was gone mad with searching. Those women saw him go with pleasure, I know it. They hated him. They said Let him return back to white-rule South Africa, where he was reared amidst snakes.

Sunday Mma Wren came forth at sunrise to awaken them. She was quiet, no longer raging and hard. She said they must not go to church, but rather aid her in some task of importance. She said We must not store up possessions in our life, as you can find in scripture. She said you must give your goods out. She said I am punished, now I must do it.

So at once she carried out countless things to set before those women, saying to take them from the face of the earth. At times she would bear many items to them, as towels and cushions. At times she would carry them one item, down to a spoon. Those maids say they warned against it many times, but failed, but yet why did they summon friends to come from nearby? Food was carried out. Goods flew like sand across the fence: shoes, knives, a clock. At every turn, the women said Is it your order that we take this thing away? and always she agreed. They are clever. Some guys who came said to Mma Wren, Can you carry me some tools, Mma? But those maids crushed them to silence. They said No one shall ask any goods beforehand. They said She is serving God in this way.

Those women are of differing churches. Sunday one pastor came, and then another, seeking gifts for God. One came with men for bearing loads. There are many tales of men swiftly bearing off chairs and tables with no one hailing them to say, What! It is because they are clever and went by the back paths and not where cars could mark them. And much was taken as from Monday, very early, before Europeans rise and see from their windows. A pastor came to thank Mma Wren for helping Africans with enriching of their churches so as to gain level some day with Europeans, because without such aid they must always remain poor.

The end of taking goods came about. Some women of one church saw too many prizes falling to another church, and grew jealous. Always if you ring up the police they can say you must come for us, for our transport is gone out. So then one woman went to them by foot to force them to return back with her. And so it was all ended.

Bastiaan was returned back with Rra Wren. He was

shamed. He became cruel. Soon Mma Wren was taken off. They said she must stay at a house of rest at Bloemfontein. Bastiaan said we may not see her face, we are unworthy, we must be driven out from that place. All power was with Bastiaan, as Rra Wren must go to join Mma Wren on leave for a time. When he could return back, we could not know, we are too lowly, and culprits.

At last Bastiaan summoned me. I said What have I done that is wrong? But Bastiaan said that only because I was absent I was no better than the others. He said there was no more a place for me there. He said I was hired on to cater for Mma Wren, in fact, because she favored me. I saw my crime of thieving was unknown. He cursed all staff and even fell to naming tribes for shortcomings. I was crying. Those women begged mercy of Bastiaan, yet still lashed him with words in secret when he said they must depart. The officer from Labor came and said Clear off as this man tells you, and be glad of his Christian heart to prevent you from jail. Then those women were raging as to reference letter they must be provided. And Bastiaan said Go to your *moruti*, your thief-pastor, and let him write for you and all others in your thief-churches, but never come to me with this matter. They said it was revenge. Many said they would complain to heaven at the Labor Office and the Office of the President as well, but if they did this I am not sure. All were sacked.

It was at night. I was pushed out. Again I must carry my goods about, lost, like an ant searching. It was at Churchill Roundabout, where four roads go out and you see Holy Cross Cathedral of the Anglicans rising up before you.

I stood with burning eyes. Many people passed in there. Cars blocked up the verges nearby. Choirs sang hymns I knew already. I saw lights beaming on some bright things. The Anglicans are rich. You can see their priests in costly robes. Always their church is built up the highest. Over countless years these European churches saved their funds well, whilst Africans prayed in the bush, never scheming as to collections. Those Anglicans have strong-rooms.

At once I saw my onward path. I said what! I can get treasure from God's many churches. They bid you to come inside. There is always money found there. I said I can be nice, I can sing, they shall help me, even, as an orphan. I can join in choirs, I said. I can be in their bosom and then rob them freely. I can rob from collections, I said, I can rob at fêtes. At pastors' houses there is endless passing in or out of women bearing tales, and I could thus find chances there. I said I shall be God's enemy and servant both in one, and nothing shall escape my hand. I said I can go farther, to great churches beyond Botswana, where you can find crosses made from gold, and shawls and clothing all with gold. I said I can pull out every thread of gold, until God shall at last cry out He wishes me to cease.

At once my heart was light.

INSTRUMENTS OF SEDUCTION

The name she was unable to remember was torturing her. She kept coming up with Bechamel, which was ridiculously wrong yet somehow close. It was important to her that she remember: a thing in a book by this man lay at the heart of her secret career as a seducer of men, three hundred and twelve of them. She was a seducer, not a seductress. The male form of the term was active. A seductress was merely someone who was seductive and who might or might not be awarded a victory. But a seducer was a professional, a worker, and somehow a record of success was embedded in the term. "Seducer" sounded like a credential. Game was afoot tonight. Remembering the name was part of the preparation. She had always prepared before tests.

Male or female, you couldn't be considered a seducer if you were below a certain age, had great natural beauty, or if you lacked a theory of what you were doing. Her body of theory began with a scene in the book she was feeling the impulse to reread. The book's title was lost in the mists of time. As she remembered the scene, a doctor and perhaps the woman of the house are involved together in some emergency lifesaving operation. The woman has to assist. The setting is an apartment in Europe, in a city. The woman is not attractive. The doctor is. There has been shelling or an accident. The characters are disparate in every way and would never normally be appropriate for one another. The operation is described in upsetting detail. It's touch and go. When it's over, the doctor and the woman fall into one another's arms—to their own surprise. Some fierce tropism compels them. Afterward they part, never to follow up. The book was from the French. She removed the Atmos clock from the living room mantel and took it to the pantry to get it out of sight.

The scene had been like a flashbulb going off. She had realized that, in her seductions up to that point, she had been crudely and intuitively using the principle that the scene made explicit. Putting it bluntly, a certain atmosphere of allusion to death, death-fear, death threats, mystery pointing to death was, in the right hands, erotic and could lead to a bingo. Of course, that was hardly all there was to it. The subject of what conditions conduce—that was her word for it—to achieving a bingo was immense. For example, should you strew your conversation with a few petals of French? The answer was not always yes, and depended on age and educational level. For some older types, France meant looseness and Pigalle. But for some it meant you were parading your education or your travel opportunities. One thing, it was never safe to roll your *R*s. She thought, Everything counts: chiaroscuro, no giant clocks in evidence and no wristwatches either, music or its absence, what they can assume about privacy and *le futur*. That was critical. You had to help them intuit you were acting from appetite, like a man, and that when it was over you would be yourself and not transformed before their eyes into a love-leech, a limbless tube of longing. You had to convince them that what was to come was, no question about it, a transgression, but that for you it was about at the level of eating between meals.

She was almost fifty. For a woman, she was old to be a seducer. The truth was that she had been on the verge of closing up shop. The corner of Bergen County they had lived

in was scorched earth, pretty much. Then Frank had been
offered a contract to advise African governments on dental
care systems. They had come to Africa for two years.

In Botswana, where they were based, everything was
unbelievably conducive. Frank was off in the bush or advising as far away as Lusaka or Gwelo for days and sometimes
weeks at a time. So there was space. She could select. Gaborone was comfortable enough. And it was full of transient
men: consultants, contractors, travelers of all kinds, seek-
ers. Embassy men were assigned for two-year tours and
knew they were going to be rotated away from the scene of
the crime sooner rather than later. Wives were often absent.
Either they were slow to arrive or they were incessantly away
on rest and recreation in the United States or the Republic
of South Africa. For expatriate men, the local women were a
question mark. Venereal disease was pandemic, and local
attitudes toward birth control came close to being surreal.
She had abstained from Batswana men. She knew why. The
very attractive ones seemed hard to get at. There was a
feeling of danger in the proposition, probably irrational. The
surplus of more familiar white types was a simple fact. In
any case, there was still time. This place had been designed
with her in mind. The furniture the government provided
even looked like it came from a bordello. And Botswana was
unnerving in some overall way there was only one word for:
conducive. The country depended on copper and diamonds.
Copper prices were sinking. There were too many diamonds
of the wrong kind. Development projects were going badly
and making people look bad, which made them nervous and
susceptible. What was there to do at night? There was only
one movie house in town. The movies came via South Africa
and were censored to a fare-thee-well—no nudity, no blue
language. She suspected that for American men the kind of
heavy-handed dummkopf censorship they sat through at the

Capitol Cinema was in fact stimulating. Frank was getting United States Government money, which made them semi-official. She had to admit there was fun in foiling the eyes and ears of the embassy network. She would hate to leave.

Only one thing was sad. There was no one she could tell about her life. She had managed to have a remarkable life. She was ethical. She never brought Frank up or implied that Frank was the cause in any way of what she chose to do. Nor would she ever seduce a man who could conceivably be a recurrent part of Frank's life or sphere. She assumed feminists would hate her life if they knew. She would like to talk to feminists about vocation, about goal-setting, about using one's mind, about nerve and strength. Frank's ignorance was one of her feats. How many women could do what she had done? She was modestly endowed and now she was even old. She was selective. Sometimes she felt she would like to tell Frank, when it was really over, and see what he said. She would sometimes let herself think he would be proud, in a way, or that he could be convinced he should be. There was no one she could tell. Their daughter was a cow and a Lutheran. Her gentleman was late. She went into the pantry to check the time.

For this evening's adventure she was conceivably a little too high-priestess, but the man she was expecting was not a subtle person. She was wearing a narrowly cut white silk caftan, a seed-pod necklace, and sandals. The symbolism was a little crude: silk, the ultracivilized material, over the primitive straight-off-the-bush necklace. Men liked to feel things through silk. But she wore silk as much for herself as for the gentlemen. Silk energized her. She loved the feeling of silk being slid up the backs of her legs. Her nape hairs rose a little as she thought about it. She had her hair up, in a loose, flat bun. She was ringless. She had put on and then taken off her scarab ring. Tonight she wanted the feeling that bare hands and bare feet would give. She would ease off her sandals at the right moment. She knew she was giving up a proven piece of business—idly taking off her ring when the occasion reached a certain centigrade. Men saw it subliminally as taking off a wedding ring and as the first act in undressing. She had worked hard on her feet. She had lined her armpits with tissue that would stay just until the doorbell rang. With medical gentlemen, hygiene was a fetish. She was expecting a doctor. Her breath was immaculate. She was proud of her teeth, but then she was married to a dentist. She thought about the Danish surgeon who brought his own boiled-water ice cubes to cocktail parties. She had some bottled water in the refrigerator, just in case it was indicated.

Her gentleman was due and overdue. Everything was optimal. There was a firm crossbreeze. The sight lines were nice. From where they would be sitting they would look out at a little pad of healthy lawn, the blank wall of the inner court, and the foliage of the tree whose blooms still looked to her like scrambled eggs. It would be self-evident that they would be private here. The blinds were drawn. Everything was secure and cool. Off the hall leading to the bathroom, the door to the bedroom stood open. The bedroom was clearly a working bedroom, not taboo, with a nightlight on and an oscillating fan performing on low. He would sit on leather; she would sit half-facing, where she could reach the bar trolley, on sheepskin, her feet on a jennet-skin kaross. He should sit in the leather chair because it was regal but uncomfortable. You would want to lie down. She would be in a slightly more reclining mode. Sunset was on. Where was her gentleman? The light was past its peak.

The doorbell rang. Be superb, she thought.

The doctor looked exhausted. He was gray-faced. Also, he was older than the image of him she had been entertaining.

But he was all right. He had nice hair. He was fit. He might be part Indian, with those cheekbones and being from Vancouver. Flats were never a mistake. He was not tall. He was slim.

She led him in. He was wearing one of the cheaper safari suits, with the *S*-for-something embroidery on the left breast pocket. He had come straight from work, which was in her favor.

When she had him seated, she said, "Two slight catastrophes to report, doctor. One is that you're going to have to eat appetizers from my own hand. As the British say, my help are gone. My cook and my maid are sisters. Their aunt died. For the second time, actually. Tebogo is forgetful. In any case, they're in Mochudi for a few days and I'm alone. Frank won't be home until Sunday. *And,* the Webers are off for tonight. They can't come. We're on our own. I hope we can cope."

He smiled weakly. The man was exhausted.

She said, "But a cool drink, quick, wouldn't you say? What would you like? I have everything."

He said it should be anything nonalcoholic, any kind of juice would be good. She could see work coming. He went to wash up.

He took his time in the bathroom, which was normally a good sign. He looked almost crisp when he came back, but something was the matter. She would have to extract it.

He accepted iced rooibos tea. She poured Bombay gin over crushed ice for herself. Men noticed what you drank. This man was not strong. She was going to have to underplay.

She presented the appetizers, which were genius. You could get through a week on her collations if you needed to, or you could have a few select tastes and go on to gorge elsewhere with no one the wiser. But you would remember every bite. She said, "You might like these. These chunks

are bream fillet, poached, from Lake Ngami. No bones. Vin-
aigrette. They had just started getting these down here on a
regular basis on ice about a year ago. AID had a lot of money
in the Lake Ngami fishery project. Then the drought struck,
and Lake Ngami, pouf, it's a damp spot in the desert. This
is real Parma ham. I nearly had to kill someone to get it.
The cashews are a little on the tangy side. That's the way
they like them in Mozambique, apparently. They're good."

· He ate a little, sticking to mainstream items like the
gouda cheese cubes, she was sorry to see. Then he brought
up the climate, which made her writhe. It was something to
be curtailed. It led the mind homeward. It was one of the
three deadly *W*s: weather, wife, and where to eat—in this
country, where not to eat. She feigned sympathy. He was
saying he was from British Columbia so it was to be expected
that it would take some doing for him to adjust to the dry
heat and the dust. He said he had to remind himself that
he'd been here only four months and that ultimately his
mucous membrane system was supposed to adapt. But he
said he was finding it wearing. Lately he was dreaming about
rain, a lot, he said.

Good! she thought. "Would you like to see my *tokoloshi*?" she asked, crossing her legs.

He stopped chewing. She warned herself not to be reck-
less.

"Dream animals!" she said. "Little effigies. I collect
them. The Bushmen carve them out of softwood. They
use them as symbols of evil in some ceremony they do.
They're turning up along with all the other Bushman artifacts, the puberty aprons and so on, in the craft shops. Let
me show you."

She got two *tokoloshi* from a cabinet.

"They call these the evil creatures who come to you at
night in dreams. There are some interesting features. What

you see when you look casually is this manlike figure with what looks like the head of a fox or rabbit or zebra at first glance. But look at the clothing. Doesn't this look like a clerical jacket? The collar shape? They're all like that. And look closely at the animal. It's actually a spotted jackal, the most despised animal there is because of its taste for carrion. Now look in front at this funny little tablet that looks like a huge belt buckle with these X shapes burned into it. My theory is that it's a Bushman version of the Union Jack. If you notice on this one, the being is wearing a funny belt. It looks like a cartridge belt to me. Some of the *tokoloshi* are smoking these removable pipes. White tourists buy these things and think they're cute. I think each one is a carved insult to the West. And we buy loads of them. I do. The black areas like the jacket are done by charring the wood with hot nails and things."

He handled the carvings dutifully and then gave them back to her. He murmured that they were interesting.

He took more tea. She stood the *tokoloshi* on an end table halfway across the room, facing them. He began contemplating them, sipping his tea minutely. Time was passing. She had various mottoes she used on herself. One was, Inside every suit and tie is a naked man trying to get out. She knew they were stupid, but they helped. He was still in the grip of whatever was bothering him.

"I have something that might interest you," she said. She went to the cabinet again and returned with a jackal-fur wallet, which she set down on the coffee table in front of him. "This is a fortune-telling kit the witch doctors use. It has odd things inside it." He merely looked at it.

"Look inside it," she said.

He picked it up reluctantly and held it in his hand, making a face. He was thinking it was unsanitary. She was in danger of becoming impatient. The wallet actually was slightly fetid, but so what: it was an organic thing. It was old.

She reached over and guided him to open and empty the wallet, touching his hands. He studied the array of bones and pebbles on the tabletop. Some of the pebbles were painted or stained. The bones were knucklebones, probably opossum, she told him, after he showed no interest in trying to guess what they were. She had made it her business to learn a fair amount about Tswana divination practices, but he wasn't asking. He moved the objects around listlessly.

She lit a candle, though she felt it was technically premature. It would give him something else to stare at if he wanted to, and at least he would be staring in her direction, more or less.

The next segment was going to be taxing. The pace needed to be meditative. She was fighting impatience.

She said, "Africa is so strange. You haven't been here long, but you'll see. We come here as . . . bearers of science, the scientific attitude. Even the dependents do, always telling the help about nutrition and weaning and that kind of thing.

"Science so much defines us. One wants to be scientific, or at least not *un*scientific. Science is our religion, in a way. Or at least you begin to feel it is. I've been here nineteen months . . ."

He said something. Was she losing her hearing or was the man just unable to project? He had said something about noticing that the *tokoloshi* weren't carrying hypodermic needles. He was making the point, she guessed, that the Batswana didn't reject Western medicine. He said something further about their attachment to injections, how they felt you weren't actually treating them unless they could have an injection, how they seemed to love injections. She would have to adapt to a certain lag in this man's responses. I am tiring, she thought.

She tried again, edging her chair closer to his. "Of course, your world is different. You're more insulated at the Ministry, where everyone is a scientist of sorts. You're immersed in science. That world is . . . safer. Are you following me?"

He said that he wasn't sure that he was.

"What I guess I mean is that one gets to want to really *uphold* science. Because the culture here is so much the opposite. So relentlessly so. You resist. But then the first thing you know, very peculiar things start happening to you. Or you talk to some of the old-settler types, whites, educated people from the Protectorate days who decided to stay on as citizens, before the government made that such an obstacle course. The white settlers are worse than your everyday Batswana. They accept everything supernatural, almost. At first you dismiss it as a pose."

She knew it was strictly pro forma, but she offered him cigarettes from the caddy. He declined. There was no way she could smoke, then. Nothing tonight was going to be easy. Bechamel was right next door to the name she was trying to remember: Why couldn't she get it?

"But it isn't a pose," she said. "Their experiences have changed them utterly. There is so much witchcraft. It's called *muti*. It's so routine. It wasn't so long ago that if you were going to open a business you'd go to the witch doctor for good luck rites with human body parts as ingredients. A little something to tuck under the cornerstone of your bottle store. People are still being killed for their parts. It might be a windpipe or whatever. It's still going on. Sometimes they dump the body onto the railroad tracks after they've taken what they need, for the train to grind up and disguise. Recently they caught somebody that way. The killers threw this body on the track but the train was late. They try to keep it out of the paper, I know that for a fact. But it's still happening. An undertow."

She worked her feet out of her sandals. Normally she would do one and let an intriguing gap fall before doing the other. She scratched an instep on an ankle.

She said, "I know a girl who's teaching in the government secondary in Bobonong who tells me what a hard time the matron is having getting the girls to sleep with their heads out of the covers. It seems they're afraid of *bad women* who roam around at night, who'll scratch their faces. These are women called *baloi,* who go around naked, wearing only a little belt made out of human neckbones. Naturally, anyone would say what a fantasy this is. Childish.

"But I really did once see a naked woman dodging around near some rondavels late one night, out near Mosimane. It was only a glimpse. No doubt it was innocent. But she did have something white and shimmering around her waist. We were driving past. You begin to wonder."

She waited. He was silent.

"Something's bothering you," she said.

He denied it.

She said, "At any rate, don't you think it's interesting that there are no women members of the so-called traditional doctors' association? I know a member, what an oaf! I think it's a smoke-screen association. They want you to think they're just a benign bunch of herbalists trying out one thing or another, a lot of which ought to be in the regular pharmacopeia if only white medical people weren't so narrow-minded. They come to seminars all jolly and humble. But if you talk to the Batswana, you know that it's the women, the witches, who are the really potent ones."

Still he was silent.

"Something's happened, hasn't it? To upset you. If it's anything I've said, please tell me." A maternal tone could be death. She was flirting with failure.

He denied that she was responsible in any way. It

seemed sincere. He was going inward again, right before her
eyes. She had a code name for failures. She called them
case studies. Her attitude was that every failure could be
made to yield something of value for the future. And it was
true. Some of her best material, anecdotes, references to
things, aphrodisiana of all kinds, had come from case studies. The cave paintings at Gargas, in Spain, of mutilated
hands . . . hand prints, not paintings . . . stencils of hun-
dreds of hands with joints and fingers missing. Archaeolo-
gists were totally at odds as to what all that meant. One case
study had yielded the story of fat women in Durban buying
tainted meat from butchers so as to contract tapeworms for
weight loss purposes. As a case study, if it came to that,
tonight looked unpromising. But you could never tell. She
had an image for case studies: a grave robber, weary, exhausted, reaching down into some charnel mass and pulling
up a lovely ancient sword somehow miraculously still keen
that had been overlooked. She could name case studies that
were more precious to her than bingoes she could describe.

She had one quiver left. She meant arrow. She hated
using it.

She could oppose her silence to his until he broke. It
was difficult to get right. It ran counter to being a host, being
a woman, and to her own nature. The silence had to be
special, not wounded, receptive, with a spine to it, maternal, in fact.

She declared silence. Slow moments passed.

He stirred. His lips stirred. He got up and began pacing.

He said, "You're right." Then for a long time he said
nothing, still pacing.

"You read my mind!" he said. "Last night I had an experience . . . I still . . . it's still upsetting. I shouldn't have
come, I guess."

She felt sorry for him. He had just the slightest speech defect, which showed up in noticeable hesitations. This was sad.

"Please tell me about it," she said perfectly.

He paced more, then halted near the candle and stared at it.

"I hardly drink," he said. "Last night was an exception. Phoning home to Vancouver started it, domestic nonsense. I won't go into that. They don't understand. No point in going into it. I went out. I went drinking. One of the hotel bars, where Africans go. I began drinking. I was drinking and buying drinks for some of the locals. I drank quite a bit.

"All right. These fellows are clever. Bit by bit I am being taken over by one, this one fellow, George. I can't explain it. I didn't like him. He took me over. That is, I notice I'm paying for drinks but this fellow's passing them on to whomever he chooses, his friends. But I'm buying. But I have no say.

"We're in a corner booth. It's dark and loud, as usual. This fellow, his head was shaved, he was strong-looking. He spoke good English, though. Originally, I'd liked talking to him, I think. They flatter you. He was a combination of rough and smooth. Now he was working me. He was a refugee from South Africa, that always starts up your sympathy. Terrible breath, though. I was getting a feeling of something being off about the ratio between the number of drinks and what I was laying out. I think he was taking something in transit.

"I wanted to do the buying. I took exception. All right. Remember that they have me wedged in. That was stupid, but I was, I allowed it. Then I said I was going to stop buying. George didn't like it. This man had a following. I realized they were forming a cordon, blocking us in. Gradually it got nasty. Why wouldn't I keep buying drinks, didn't

I have money, what was my job, didn't the Ministry pay expatriates enough to buy a few drinks?—so on ad nauseam."

His color was coming back. He picked up a cocktail napkin and touched at his forehead.

He was looking straight at her now. He said, "You don't know what the African bars are like. Pandemonium. I was sealed off. As I say, his friends were all around.

"Then it was all about apartheid. I said I was Canadian. Then it was about Canada the lackey of America the supporter of apartheid. I'm not political. I was scared. All right. When I tell him I'm really through buying drinks he asks me how much money have I got left, exactly. I tell him again that I'm through buying drinks. He says not to worry, he'll sell me something instead. All right. I knew I was down to about ten pula. And I had dug in on buying drinks, the way you will when you've had a few too many. No more buying drinks, that was decided. But he was determined to get my money, I could damned well see that.

"He said he would sell me something I'd be very glad to know. Information. All right. So then comes a long runaround on what kind of information. Remember that he's pretty well three sheets to the wind himself. It was information I would be glad to have as a doctor, he said.

"Well, the upshot here was that this is what I proposed, so as not to seem totally stupid and taken. I would put all my money down on the table in front of me. I took out my wallet and made sure he could see that what I put down was all of it, about ten pula, change and everything. All right. And I would keep the money under the palm of my hand. And he would whisper the information to me and if I thought it was a fair trade I would just lift my hand. Of course, this was all just face-saving on my part so as not to just hand over my money to a thug. And don't think I wasn't well aware it might be a good idea at this stage of things to be seen getting rid of any cash I had, just to avoid being knocked down on the way to my car."

"This is a wonderful story," she said spontaneously, immediately regretting it.

"It isn't a story," he said.

"You know what I mean," she said. "I mean, since I see you standing here safe and sound I can assume the ending isn't a tragedy. But please continue. Really."

"In any event. There we are. There was more back and forth over what kind of information this was. Finally he says it's not only something a doctor would be glad of. He is going to tell me the secret of how they are going to make the revolution in South Africa, a secret plan. An actual plan.

"God knows I have no brief for white South Africans. I know a few professionally, doctors. Medicine down there is basically about up to 1950, in my opinion, despite all this veneer of the heart transplants. But the doctors I know seem to be decent. Some of them hate the system and will say so.

"I go along. Empty my wallet, cover the money with my hand.

"Here's what he says. They had a sure way to drive out the whites. It was a new plan and was sure to succeed. It would succeed because they, meaning the blacks, could bring it about with only a handful of men. He said that the Boers had won for all time if the revolution meant waiting for small groups to grow into bands and then into units, battalions and so on, into armies that would fight the Boers. The Boers were too intelligent and had too much power. They had corrupted too many of the blacks. The blacks were divided. There were too many spies for the Boers among them. The plan he would tell me would take less than a hundred men.

"Then he asked me, if he could tell me such a plan

would it be worth the ten pula. Would I agree that it would? I said yes."

"This is extraordinary!" she said. *Duhamel!* she thought, triumphant. The name had come back to her: *Georges Duhamel.* She could almost see the print. She was so grateful.

"Exciting!" she said, gratitude in her voice.

He was sweating. "Well, this is what he says. He leans over, whispers. The plan is simple. The plan is to assemble a shock force, he called it. Black people who are willing to give their lives. And this is all they do: *they kill doctors.* That's it! They start off with a large first wave, before the government can do anything to protect doctors. They simply kill doctors, as many as they can. They kill them at home, in their offices, in hospitals, in the street. You can get the name of every doctor in South Africa through the phone book. Whites need doctors, without doctors they think they are already dying, he says. Blacks in South Africa have no doctors to speak of anyway, especially in the homelands where they are all being herded to die in droves. Blacks are dying of the system every day regardless, he says. But whites would scream. They would rush like cattle to the airports, screaming. They would stream out of the country. The planes from Smuts would be jammed full. After the first strike, you would continue, taking them by ones and twos. The doctors would leave, the ones who were still alive. No new ones would come, not even Indians. He said it was like taking away water from people in a desert. The government would capitulate. That was the plan.

"I lifted my hand and let him take the money. He said I was paying the soldiery, and he thanked me in the name of the revolution. Then I was free to go."

He looked around dazedly for something, she wasn't clear what. Her glass was still one third full. Remarkably, he picked it up and drained it, eating the remnants of ice.

She stood up. She was content. The story was a brilliant thing, a gem.

He was moving about. It was hard to say, but possibly he was leaving. He could go or stay.

They stood together in the living room archway. Without prelude, he reached for her, awkwardly pulled her side against his chest, kissed her absurdly on the eye, and with his free hand began squeezing her breasts.

OFFICIAL AMERICANS

It was the next day.

Not a moment too soon, Carl thought, exhausted. He watched the corona brighten around the drawn curtains. Hot light was flooding Africa one more time. His days were like nights and his nights were like days, because of the dogs. He got his rest during the day—in increments, in stolen naps at his desk or in the car, or at lunchtime at home. His days were dim, like dreams. His nights were war. The dogs began barking every night at seven, or when he went to bed, whichever came first. There were eleven dogs in the yard next door. The furor kept up until daybreak, except for weekends, when—he'd be willing to swear—it went on even later. When he came home for lunch, the dogs were laid out around Letsamao's yard like slugs or duffel bags, sleeping in the sun—filling up with sleep.

He inched himself up into a sitting position and looked down at his sleeping darling. They had been married less than a year. Sometimes she smiled in her sleep. He loved her teeth, small and white, like mints. He had all his teeth, knock wood. Lois was twenty-eight and he was fifty-six. She was his second wife, and she was perfect. Her skin was perfect for Africa—the way she tanned beautifully. She loved Botswana's dry climate, and in fact that reminded him to remind her to be sensitive about the drought when she was enthusing about the climate in front of people. He loved her all the time. She was grateful for everything. He had saved her from Oregon, she liked to say. She meant the climate and what it had done to her sinuses. She meant her job as a cashier in a hotel restaurant in Medford, where they had met when he was on vacation recuperating from his breakup with Elaine. Lois was unmarried when he met her, because she had been waiting for two key things in one: a man she could respect, who was also someone not fated to live in Oregon forever because of his work or family ties. She thought that his job with the Agency for International Development was wonderful, because it kept him in sunny countries and it helped the poor. She thought of AID as something like the Red Cross. She was a wonderful specimen. She was improving his life in so many ways that he couldn't keep up with it. His salt intake was down, due to her tricks with lemon juice and so on. Also, he had always thought of hair spray as effeminate and had preferred to duck out and comb his hair nineteen times a day, with water if need be, rather than use it. But then she had shown him that the hair sprays he had tried were too strong and made his hair look like icing, and she had gotten him one that was the right strength and now his hair was fine all day and could be forgotten about. She was a helpmeet: his first. She could be an ad for health food, she looked so well. She could sleep almost at will, it seemed to him. She invariably slept through the dogs. They couldn't keep her awake. He kept her awake, if he was restless, but not the dogs themselves.

He lowered one foot to the floor. It was amazing to him how much he wanted to be fit, these days. Of course, anyone with a young wife would want to be fit, to some extent. That was why the thing with the dogs had to be brought to an end. But his attitude toward being in shape was a hundred per cent the reverse of what it had been under Elaine, if that was the right way to put it. His attitude toward jogging was a case in point. Jogging had been invented while his back was turned—while he was in Malawi or Togo, probably. He could remember that the first time he had seen joggers, when he and Elaine had been back in New York on home leave—in an expensive hotel, naturally, on Central Park South—it was already a mass movement. Elaine had been a genius at choosing the most expensive city or country for rest and recreation. If there were two countries, one where the dollar was high and the other where it was really low, there would always be a compelling reason to go where it was most expensive. It had to be France because the springs under the Fontaine de Vaucluse were drying up, or it had to be Italy because the Villa d'Este was closing down its most unique fountains because a tire factory was polluting the water. So, there he had been, looking out the window down into beautiful, green Central Park and seeing joggers everywhere. Now he saw the point of it—he himself was walking everywhere he could—but at the time he had been able to see the joggers only as something interrupting his pleasure in looking at the park, something agitating, something that marred the beauty of the vegetation, like aphids. Lo had information about health. People were amazed when she proved to them that some salt companies were adding sugar, or some form of it, to salt.

He was up. He felt fragile, because of the dogs. By rights, he should be feeling reborn, almost. He was hardly drinking. There was Lo. He was basically through with smoking. But he felt fragile. Botswana felt dangerous to him. For instance, the floor beneath his feet. The Batswana kept waxing, no matter what was said to them. Lo was too soft. Overwaxing was still going on. At work, the cleaners waxed directly on bare concrete, on stoops, on steps. The floors blazed everywhere. They could kill you. Barefoot was safest. Thongs were dangerous on these floors.

There was one other thing that not sleeping was making him irrational on: the geyser. He tried not to be. But the hot water for the tub and shower came from a gigantic cylinder bolted to the wall above the bathtub, with electric coils in a collar at its base. It would crush anyone in the tub if it ever came loose from its moorings. And Lo took baths, exclusively. He was always obsessively inspecting the geyser, pulling at the mountings and feeling at the same time that he might be weakening the thing with all his testing. Hot baths were therapy for Lo. The giant tubs the British had established as normal all over Africa were a revelation to her. The shower stall was separate and safe.

He set the shower to spray just enough to get him rinsed but not enough to bother Lo. He was expert at showering quietly. He was used to the African workday starting when it did—ungodly early. She was still adapting. He liked her to sleep late. Small things about her made him emotional, like lying about her age to make herself older and more appropriate for him when they were courting. That was the kind of thing he loved. Or, recently, when he'd said he felt like Prometheus having his liver torn out every night and regenerating each day so it could be torn out again the next night, and she'd asked who Prometheus was. The hot water directly on his scalp was helping.

Walking was calming, and Carl liked the half-mile walk from his office to the medical unit. The embassy nurse wanted to see him. He knew he was overdue for his gamma globulin, but there was something more she wanted to discuss. He was going to plead with her for a state-of-the-art sleeping pill. He wouldn't get it: she was to the right of medically conservative. The regular pills were no help. They would knock him out but not keep him out. Lo's prescription for him was more exercise, as in jogging. The thought was torture. He was too tired for exercise. In any case, the problem wasn't falling asleep, it was getting back to sleep once the Minister of Labor's dogs started their demented crooning and baying and snarling and fighting or mating or tunneling under the fence to come skulking around the house, rifling his trash cans.

In Gaborone, when he walked, he used the network of dirt paths behind the houses—the "people's paths." Africa was humanity walking, or rather Africans walking. Whites rode. He was almost the only white ambulating along with the Batswana. People looked at him. It would be fair to say they stared. They were staring now, a little. He thought, They can't get over my uncanny resemblance to Samuel Beckett. Immediately, he felt guilty. He did look like Beckett, but the thought was bad—the kind of thing Elaine would have broken up over. There were plenty of reasons to stare at him. He was tall and so forth. He remembered about his posture and straightened up. This part of Gaborone was like a university town someplace in the American Southwest, except for the walls and fences around the house plots. He had been in Africa so long that residential neighborhoods in America looked utopian—no property-line fencing to speak of, people's lawns intermingling.

He should enjoy nature more. There were a lot of gum trees on this route. There were other trees whose blooms looked like scrambled eggs. Lo noticed everything. The first time she'd seen him naked she'd noticed that his right arm was permanently darkened by the sun, from the elbow down, from having it out the window as he drove around Africa on site visits. Sometimes Lo said his name in her sleep. It moved him enormously. It was proof of something. He doubted Elaine had ever talked in her sleep. But how would he know, because in those days he slept at night, and Elaine was on her guard to the roots of her being. Lo wanted him to show more interest in the local birdlife. He thought, When it comes to bird-watching, I say let the birds watch *me*. A colony of Cape vultures had a nesting ground in the cliffs near Ootse. There was supposedly a trail up the cliffs, so that interested parties could get close enough to look directly at the vultures or even interfere with them. Lo wanted to go. He might be able to manage that.

Just ahead, at the edge of the path, was a fruit stand—two upended cartons. The vendor was a Motswana matron wearing a housedress and a blanket over it like an apron. He was going to be irritated, he could tell. He stopped to look over the display of bananas and green apples. The fruit was less than fresh—probably it had been four or five days on the street already. Batswana merchants absolutely would not bargain. This woman needed to clear her stock. She should lower her prices drastically, for the bananas at least. But she had her unit price figured and would stick to it unto death. She knew what the other street vendors were getting and would consider she was being made a fool of if she took less. If he offered a lower price, she would think he was trying to take advantage of her. He had been through this. The fruit came from South Africa and was substandard to begin with—*ondergraad*. The Batswana wholesalers were stuck with long-term contracts for fruit the South Africans wouldn't touch. He knew all about it. It was a scandal.

The vendor waited for him to say something. She decided to eat an apple. He predicted that she would take one of the best ones, not one of the least salable, and she did. Sometimes he thought southern Africa was specially designed to try the souls of small-business experts. He had had his difficulties persuading Africans elsewhere in the continent to be serious about business, but southern Africa was the sharpest thorn in his crown so far. He had to give himself mixed reviews at best for his performance to date—for his career—so he had to succeed in Botswana. This was not the best subject vis-à-vis his blood pressure. Botswana was probably his last chance to stay overseas. He ought to be able to succeed, because his main project was foolproof: it was all women, very tractable, making school uniforms for a guaranteed market—the state.

The settlement with Elaine had impoverished him. Because of Lois, he had to be overseas to recoup, because the housing and utilities were covered and they could save like bandits. If they demoted him back to Washington, he and Lo would end up living like graduate students—at that level. Lo would have to go out and cashier. It was unthinkable. Since he'd stopped, he had to buy something from this woman. He paid twenty *thebe* for a banana—four *thebe* more than his highest estimate. Still, the woman was looking implacably at him. What had he done? It came to him: he had forgotten to greet her before starting the transaction. That made him a worm, in her eyes. He moved on.

Secretaries and technical personnel tended to live at the embassy compound, a square of apartments around a microscopic swimming pool. One apartment had been turned over to the nurse, for a medical unit. In a previous incarnation he would have been interested in the nurse, Rita. She was single. She was low-forties and Hispanic, and tough. He liked lean women. He looked at the empty pool wrinkling and creasing in the noon sun. There was a woman he had read about, a prodigy, nineteenth century, who could sleep floating in water. It might have been a man. There had been two prodigies, one of them named Fraticoni, and one was the Human Magnet and metal objects stuck to him or her, and the other was the Human Cork, who could sleep floating.

The nurse was steely. This was a lecture. "I'm not giving you any sleeping medication," she said. "I don't trust you around medication. You scared us with your X ray. We don't need this. You showed four strange round spots in your gastric region which we finally figured out had to be mineral-supplement pills with a lot of iron in them you weren't absorbing. Does anybody at your house know what vitaminosis is? Maybe you can't sleep because you're irritating your nervous system yourself with whatever you're taking. If you want to self-medicate, then self-medicate, but don't come to me looking for sympathy." There was more. Did he know too much niacin could turn his face red? Was he aware that it was natural for the body to require less sleep as it aged? He used to think Rita liked him.

"And *also*, I never want to find you in my office when I walk in," she said. "I don't want to make a big issue. But you sit in the waiting area, period."

"I was looking for you," Carl said. The nurse began writing. Stepping into her office when he saw it was empty had been the latest in a recent line of bright ideas. He was having too many bright ideas. He had foreseen not getting pills. The possibility that he might spot some lying around loose in the empty office had suggested itself. Then there had been a vague idea that he might be able to do something against the dogs with a syringe, if he had a syringe. He had seen disposable hypodermics in Rita's wastebasket more than once. One dog, a big orange bitch, seemed almost like the choirmaster of the pack. Whether dogs could die from an air-injection, he didn't know. Would it have been feasible to creep up on the bitch while she was rooting around near the fence and jab her? Probably not. He had taken a stupid chance. He felt pale.

Rita handed him the appointment card for his next shot. She reminded him to use the stress cassette she had given him, and said maybe he should try earplugs again. He got up, putting on his sunglasses. Lately his eyes were on the reddish side. The whites of Lo's eyes were clear, like stationery. There was a problem connected with sunglasses, which he had to keep in mind. Apparently, older Batswana resented sunglass-wearing. A Member of Parliament had criticized young Batswana for wearing sunglasses, because it was disrespectful to conceal your eyes when you were in conversation. It had been in the *Daily News*. There was probably no special dispensation for expatriates.

He left. Rita was dense about earplugs. From his standpoint, there were two things wrong with earplugs. He could hear through them—any that he had tried. And earplugs forced him to listen to his own heartbeat. He had a functional murmur. It was impossible not to listen for irregularities. Listening to his heartbeat was like listening to the drum in a Roman galley. He had explained all this, but she was still pushing earplugs. He forgave her. She still gave the best gamma-globulin shots in the foreign service. She always warmed up the ampule first in her bra and then had you toe-in to loosen up your gluteus muscle. The bruising was always minimal.

He was yanked from sleep. The barking was on.

Someplace he had seen a movie where the hero is dragged into the air on ropes attached to hooks in his flesh. This was similar, except that the movie ordeal had been an initiation for an English lord who wanted to be a Comanche brave for some unknown reason. So there was a point to it.

The moon was full. It would almost be worth it to be a werewolf. After all, he would have his little problem only once a month, like women. Then he could take care of Letsamao's dogs, either all at once or a few per month. But did werewolves eat dogs? He would.

Normally, he would go to mind force now. But he had given up on mind force, permanently. That was clear. Mind force was the only form of warfare that would let him lie immobile and not wake Lois up. Unfortunately, it was a delusion and stupid. He had tried hard to give mind force the benefit of the doubt. After all, there was a Russian medium who could make matchsticks hop around under a bell jar, supposedly. Poltergeist cases seemed to reduce to something real—certain adolescents sending out streams of invisible energy able to smash crockery and empty ashtrays on their parents' heads. Freud once made Jung faint through sheer hatred during an argument, according to Jung, and so on.

Doing mind force, he had imagined white fire flowing up from the root of his spine and out between his eyes, where it would take weaponlike forms and destroy the dogs. He had started out with benign visualizations, such as sleep-inducing fog banks. Then he had escalated to winged nooses, blunt instruments, and on to spikes and blades. Sometimes he had accompanied his visualizations with body English, like tensing his neck cords or clenching his teeth.

He was beginning to resent all the slow motion getting in and out of bed. He realized it was making him feel old. This time, he got out of bed normally. Lo murmured, but was asleep again by the time he had frozen. He picked up his bathrobe and went out into the breezeway to sit until daybreak.

Diabolically, the barking stopped.

Lois said good morning, startling Carl. She was in the kitchen doorway. There was something in her expression. It was possible he'd been thinking out loud about the breakfast he'd made, because, seeing it all laid out, he realized it was excessive.

"Hey, please don't interrupt me when I'm talking to myself," he said, getting a weak smile out of Lo.

There were poached eggs, four slices of toast, broiled

tomatoes, kippers, sliced peaches in *maas*, cornflakes, the last of their decent coffee. There was a reason for the extravagance. He had something urgent to get across. He felt that a leisurely breakfast would set up the right mood.

Lo excused herself. She would never come directly from bed to the breakfast table. Even if breakfast was brought to her in bed, she would insist on getting up to rinse her face before eating anything. She was inflexible about it. That was an example of what was worrying him about her. He had a feeling that she'd made up her mind to appeal to the ambassador for a change of housing. Carl had to prevent that. He had already explained why, and she had seemed to be listening. But there was a reservation in her attitude that had him worried. She had a naïve conception of the ambassador and his powers. He sensed she was planning to do something. It wasn't that Lois was aggressive by nature. Lo wasn't even a feminist. But Lois loved him, and because of the dogs she was a potential fanatic on getting assigned to another house.

They sat down together. There was no reference to the extent of the breakfast. She ate a little of everything, praising everything.

Over coffee, he began. "Lo, I need you to promise me something." He reached across the table for her hand. "I need you to swear on my life you won't go to the ambassador about our housing." She was silent. He knew that he had been right.

He explained it all again, watching his tone. There were no alternative houses to be had. The housing shortage in the capital was grave. The Government of Botswana was going so far as to turn down any project that required it to provide housing in the capital for experts. The ambassador was not a god, and he was helpless on this issue. There was no way anyone in his right mind would trade quarters with them, because everyone knew about the dogs. Americans were doubling up in houses meant for one family. Contract people were stuck in hotels for months.

She came back with her experience in hotel work. Desk clerks might say there was nothing available, but if you were important enough there would always be a room. She reminded Carl that they were official Americans in Botswana, not contract people.

He explained again that the ambassador saw himself as a new broom. Under the previous ambassador, the housing committee had been a circus, an uproar, a black mark for the ambassador when the inspectors came through. As a sign of strength, the new ambassador had killed the whole appeal process in the housing committee. Now it was policy that people took the housing they were assigned and liked it, or they were sent home.

Finally, he had to explain about Elaine and housing—something he had minimized until now. He was under an emotional injunction from Lois against speaking ill of Elaine, which he accepted. But there had to be exceptions. Elaine had made a hobby out of challenging their housing assignments. She had become notorious. It had gotten into his efficiency rating reports. In short, there was a negative history to be lived down. He recognized that Elaine had needed to assert herself as a person, under what she probably saw as difficult overseas conditions. Nevertheless, there had been a difficult result. Lois seemed to be understanding all this. He finished by saying that going to the ambassador, besides being absolutely not in their own interest, would make her look childish—like someone who couldn't appreciate facts. It would look like a tantrum.

She was unhappy, but she promised. He stood up. He was reluctant to go until she released him with some sign of forgiveness for everything.

A hornbill called in the garden. He had a thought. Lo

had no idea that the one bird he could always identify was the hornbill. He remembered the first time he had heard it, years ago in Rwanda. He had stiffened at whatever he was doing, guiltily. He always heard the harsh, drawn-out *aww* as a cry of disapproval, probably maternal. "I think that's a hornbill," he said.

She looked up, pleased. He could go.

Walking home late that evening, Carl made himself contemplate trying to see Letsamao again. He had already spoken to Letsamao, once by phone and once in person, but both times he had been too gingerly. Whether to avoid seeming neurotic or to engage Letsamao's chivalrous side, Carl had put it that it was mainly Lois who was suffering from the dogs. Both times, Letsamao had said the same things—that Carl's wife was oversensitive and would in time adapt; that the dogs were not extreme, as shown by the fact that no one else was complaining; that among the numerous Europeans who had lived in Carl's house previously there were none who had ever complained. Letsamao had as much as said that it was the business of a husband to manage a wife's problems and to avoid intruding on the valuable time of a cabinet minister. Letsamao had reacted in no way to the suggestion that he might take his dogs in at night. It was as though the suggestion hadn't even been made. Now Carl had a better and more moderate idea. It was that someone from among Letsamao's retinue—that was the wrong word and unfair—be appointed to come out and quiet the dogs when they started up. This time when he spoke to Letsamao he would bring himself into it, confessing that he was the one primarily suffering. Letsamao had dominated their earlier conversations, pressing Carl to finish his business quickly. Their second conversation had been short and sharp. When nothing resulted from the exchanges, Carl had gone over twice more, at times when he knew Letsamao was at home, only to be told each time by the maid that the Minister was not to be disturbed. Trying to relay complaints through Letsamao's domestics was a waste of time.

Letsamao was a rough customer he had a right to be afraid of. The Minister of Labor had oversight of all expatriates working in the country. Letsamao was a power in the ruling party. Moreover, he was a favorite of the AID mission director and the ambassador, largely because of a reputation as a strong administrator. Carl thought of the Batswana as an unusually agreeable people, so long as you remembered to greet them properly with *dumela*. Letsamao was atypical. He was permanently expressionless. He was short, thickly built, hard-looking. He was cicatriced, with three faint scars like cat scratches on each cheek. Carl had never seen Letsamao in casual dress.

He was approaching Letsamao's house. The gates in the high front walls were ajar. Carl had a flash of irritation. Letsamao's front yard, with its oblong of chive-green lawn, was beautifully landscaped and tended, but the backyard, which faced the front of Carl's house through a wire fence, was a wasteland of bare earth, flailing laundry, children, dog life. Servant Theatre was what Elaine had called a similar scene they had lived with briefly, in Blantyre.

The coach lights on either side of the gate came on. That meant Letsamao was expected imminently. On impulse, Carl stopped. He would wait at the gate to intercept Letsamao. He had time. It would be pleasant. Because of the drought, mosquitoes were scarce. The first stars were out, twitching.

Letsamao's silver Peugeot appeared at the bend in Sefhare Road, traveling briskly. Carl waved. The Peugeot swung toward the driveway. Carl stepped into the middle of the drive, one hand up, smiling hard. Letsamao stopped—more abruptly than he had to, Carl felt.

He went around to Letsamao's window and tapped. Letsamao sat looking at him for a moment before lowering the window very slowly halfway. Carl noted that Letsamao was playing the clutch, keeping the car moving slightly forward. Carl was off balance. He did remember to begin with *dumela*, but then he rushed. There was too much to convey. He said he was getting sick. He used the word "insomnia," which he had decided against using. When he said he thought it was time for an *indaba*, he could see Letsamao stiffen. Carl knew the term, meaning "powwow," from reading the *Rand Daily Mail*. The term was Zulu and was supposed to be lingua franca all over southern Africa—but was it? Had he patronized Letsamao?

Letsamao cut him off in a voice that was high-pitched, almost strangulated. "Mr. Schmoll, *dumela*, you must not trouble me with this matter time and again! I must have my watchdogs. In fact, my dogs are giving you protection, if you can understand, because they are alert as to your place as well. So, really, you must leave this! Because really my dogs are watching over you, yet I must feed them. Mr. Schmoll, you must consider your position." He drove on. Carl was now on Letsamao's grounds. Two yardmen, anxious, ran up to usher him out. Letsamao's last words had been spoken heavily, meaningfully.

It was dim in the police station. Why was it so damned dark in Africa, indoors, where people had to work? Carl thought of the artisan workshops in Mombasa—coffin-makers and metalsmiths laboring in cavelike slots lit by one light bulb or fluorescent tube. Maybe because people grew up in windowless rondavels, a little light seemed like a lot. The cost of electricity was probably nine-tenths of the explanation. Decent lighting would do wonders for productivity, he would bet. He ought to write something on it when this was over and he felt less half dead. There was such a thing as his career.

Carl sat down on a bench among silent Batswana. They were the poor. Some of them looked banged-up. There was no conversation. There was nothing to read. He decided that he had never seen a Motswana he would describe as nervous. The room was an oven.

An hour passed. The station commander would see him. Carl had already spoken to the charge officer, whose English was poor. Carl was hoping he had misunderstood the charge officer's advice.

But the station commander only reiterated what the charge officer had said. There were no laws to protect Carl. The barking of watchdogs could never be seen as a nuisance under the law. There was nothing in the law to limit the number of animals a man could keep on his grounds. All Carl could do was slay these dogs when they set foot on his plot. He could shoot them. But the best was to lure them with meat, and poison them—taking care that the poison was given within his plot. And it would be best if the animals, once they were slain, could be found on his plot as well, although that was sometimes difficult and was not essential. The station commander recommended an arsenic compound available from a stockist near the railway station. Carl was assured that this was a thing commonly done.

The skirl of the hot comb ceased. Carl sampled the soup Lois had made for dinner. It was dawning on him that Lois— all her sympathy *re* the dogs to the contrary notwithstanding—felt deep down that his real problem was crabbéd age. The soup was a case in point. It was dense with powdered kelp or lecithin or some other additive she'd looked up in her health library. She was doctoring his soup because he was at the outer limits of what a human being could be

expected to ingest in the form of pills. The soup had a me-
dicinal tang. He would deny it. He served the soup. Lois
came in, damp and pink, in her bathrobe. Her eyes looked
a little red. His report of the police-station incident had
obviously upset her. They sat down.

He still needed to talk about the business with the police. He couldn't believe that poisoning dogs was common-
place. On the other hand, when it came to considering such
an extreme proposition, not everybody lived next door to the
Minister of Labor.

Lo had nothing to say. Her problem was that she loved
animals. He had even caught her patting Letsamao's dogs
once or twice, when she'd found them nosing around the
house during the day.

Carl said, "And what if you poisoned some meat and it
got into the wrong hands, kids picking it up? Kids eat paint
and bark—all kinds of things. It's called pica. This soup is
delicious."

It was evident Lo wanted to change the subject. He knew
he was being compulsive. He said, "And how do you even
go about it? Do you marinate the meat in it, or do you
sprinkle it on like salt?" Lo was barely eating.

"It's ironic," he said. "Because I like dogs all right. I
had dogs as a kid. But these dogs make me physically ill,
almost, when I see them. Especially the ringleader bitch,
who's pregnant again, by the way. Her nipples stick out like
thumbs."

He had to get off the topic, and now. He was an adult
who was aware that he couldn't have everything, such as a
wife who was both cheerful and depressed on his behalf in
the same instant of time. She was still on the verge of tears.
He realized that he'd seen Lois really crying only once in
Africa, so far—when Letsamao's dogs had gotten into the
yard and torn up the parsley she'd planted. The parsley had

been dedicated to Carl, for his clotting-factor needs. She had been horrified to find that weeks could elapse without parsley showing up in the markets. She loved him. He apologized for bringing up the police nonsense again.

"It isn't that," she said, pushing her soup away, definitely crying.

She said, "Oh, Carl. It isn't about that. But, Carl, today I found out that Scott Nearing died." She waited. Her voice was faint. "I just found out that *Scott Nearing* died."

Carl said, "I don't know the name, I don't think."

She was surprised. "Well, he wrote some wonderful books with his wife, about living and diet and so forth, that I really loved. I don't even know why this upsets me and I'm crying like this. Well, he was wonderful and he was really old, about in his nineties. And he had a wonderful life in Maine. I don't know. I guess partly it's because I just found out he died a few months ago, because I'm in Africa. You can't experience your feelings for a person when they make transition at the time they do if you didn't even know about it at the time. But now Helen is all alone." Her tears coursed down.

At midnight, the dogs woke him—a trio. The barking was listless. It was the heat. Tonight it was so hot he knew he'd never get back to sleep, even if the dogs quit. He sat up slowly. Sweat crept down his sides. It was December. High summer had come.

All the windows were open, and an electric fan sent a stream of tepid air across the foot of the bed. There was an air-conditioner, but Lois was opposed to it. She had once worked for six months in an office at a desk directly under an air-conditioner, and that had been the beginning of the sinus problem, which only Botswana had ever helped. At work, he used his air-conditioner, but guiltily. Lo's point was that man had evolved without air-conditioning, and that using it had to deprive the body of some positive adaptive exercise. Her main dogma seemed to be to preserve the body's flexibility, by any means necessary. Lois fasted for a day every couple of weeks, just to be fasting and just because there had to be something in the body's capacity to adapt that would be triggered by fasting. He wouldn't relish fasting, but he could see it coming, a cloud no larger than a woman's hand. He could deal with it.

Carl got out of bed. He was going to be restless. His unhappiness was too great. He knew what he was going to have to do: because of the dogs, he was going to have to sleep alone from now on.

There had to be a good side to this, somewhere, because the pain of it was too much, and the heaviness coming into him. The only thing was that his night vision was improving, from all his creeping around in total darkness. He could get from room to room, find things, fix snacks, all in pitch blackness. It was a useless skill, unless it was rehearsal for blindness or becoming a cat burglar. Another thing was that if he slept in his study, he could work when he was awake. He could attack his paperwork arrears, which were getting to be significant. He could do anything that didn't involve noise, like typing. Visualizing himself working at night, he felt worse. Working at night was for students, the young.

In his study, Carl lay down on the couch. It was no good: he was sticking to the vinyl surface. He would have to spread towels over the cushions. Being in the study reminded him of an option he'd toyed with early on. He had thought of turning the study into a soundproof chamber, lining the walls with slabs of corkboard gotten from somewhere. That idea had broken up on the reef of ventilation. It would have been like lying in a crypt. There was no way he could have asked Lo to join him there. Now he had to get the towels.

The hinges on the linen closet needed oil. Lo was awake now. He heard her coming out into the hall, saying his name.

She found him at the closet and embraced him. He put the towels down and held her.

He told her he had decided he had to sleep in the study for the time being because he was destroying her sleep. He patted her. He could feel her nodding yes.

A queue lengthened outside the Ministry of Agriculture stand, where a hermaphrodite calf was on display. I could be an exhibit myself, Carl thought. Heat corrugated the hill view over the metal roofs of the food stalls. People could come and marvel at me for being able to stand up.

His plan for Saturday had been to sleep like the dead. But the deputy chief of mission's wife had struck by phone. Lois had been reminded about what it meant to be an official American. The ambassador wanted total attendance by official Americans at the Red Cross Fête. The D.C.M.'s wife had been blunt. The ambassador was determined that the American exhibit should take second place this year. By custom, first place always went to an African entry. The chief of station said Zambia was looking strong. Second place was between Britain and the United States. Vigorous attendance by an exhibit's nationals counted with the judges.

An unfamiliar American wife handed Carl a red, white, and blue paper shoulder sash and matching boutonniere. He was wearing a T-shirt, so he attached the rosette to a belt loop at his hip, hoping that that would be acceptable. The American pavilion was major—bigger than ever before. But Carl was picking up anxiety—two kinds of it. The Americans were worried, not by the British but by the Swedes and their Southern Cross Coffee House. Apparently, the Swedes were underpricing tortes and pastries worth a fortune in terms of ingredients, let alone labor. The Batswana were notorious for their love of sweets. The other anxiety was that a certain number of official Americans had been noticed stocking up on tortes for the freezer, until the ambassador had expressed himself on the subject. The word was that the judges were staying a little longer in the coffee house than was standard. It would be unfair if the Swedes won, because their exhibit had only two elements—the coffee house and a borehole-pump demonstration. Carl knew all about the wood-fired pump, which had a bad image among the American technical people. First of all, there was a famous fuel-wood shortage in Botswana. Secondly, even though the pump could run on low-quality coal, which was cheap in Botswana, the cost of transporting coal out into the Kalahari would be too high. America had gone with diversity—a cartoon-show tent, a used-clothes-and-white-elephant table, a fashion show, a bake table, a palmist. Somebody had traveled to the Republic and come back with sausages that could almost pass for American hot dogs. Carl had to make sure that the ambassador saw he was there. Should he go up and say it might be a good idea to charge the Swedes with dumping? He decided not to. He saluted the ambassador from a distance. Lois was around somewhere. She should be seen, too. He went to find her.

The Anglicans had set up their tombola stand in a grove of dying silver oaks. The trees were shedding: the fallen leaves were crisp, like fish bones underfoot. It was the drought. Improvised shelving, braced against a row of trees, held the tombola prizes: canned goods, sundries, Bibles, cheap plastic toys in blisterpacks, five-kilo sacks of mealie and sorghum. There was a crush around the tombola, with Lois at its heart.

Carl made his way to her side. She was a hit. Poor devils were cheering her on, like extras in a gambling movie cheering the heroine at roulette. He loved her. He touched her

shoulder. She was damp. He wanted to get her over to the
American pavilion, but she was too engrossed. She had won
a mountain of things, mostly canned. She hated canned
goods, as he recalled. He glanced at a few of the cans. Some
of the brands were extinct, he was sure. Storekeepers do-
nated their dead stock to the fête, but some of her prizes
looked as though they should have been destroyed instead.
That was a merchant for you. But getting rid of old stock was
the right thing to do. Lo had won a lifetime supply of pocket
combs for him. He let her know that he had to find someplace to sit down. She nodded, preoccupied just then with
trying to convey what chutney was to a Herero woman who
had won a jar of it. Glum Anglican Auxiliary women were
churning up the chances, probably in reaction to Lo's run of
luck. He told Lo to come to the American pavilion as soon
as she could, and to find a kid to carry her prizes to the car.
Carl said he was going to America, and left.

In the American pavilion, the mood was poor. The
judges had been cursory. People were saying the ambassador
was annoyed. One of the judges was Letsamao. Carl thanked
God he had been elsewhere during the judging. He needed
to sit down, badly. He considered the cartoon tent. He put
his head inside and saw that he would be the only adult. He
backed out. There was another tent, smaller, pitched outside
the main circuit of stalls and exhibits. The sign above the
door flap said "Your Fate," the letters formed by handprints in different colors. From a marketing standpoint, the
sign was dubious: it was hard to read, because the lighter-
colored handprints broke up some of the letters, and there
was no price posted. The palmist would be wondering where
her trade was. He went in. There was a chair, an armchair.

The interior was candlelit. The atmosphere was dark
yellow. The palmist was a woman his age. She was seated
behind a table draped with a kaross. He knew who she was:
she was the wife of their dental-systems man, Napier. Carl

knew something about her and tried to remember what it was. There was some kind of feeling against her among the wives, except for Lo as per usual. As he recalled, people said she had something to do with the occult. Her name was Ione, he knew. She had gone all out. Her lean face was masklike with powder, and her eyes were extreme—framed in squared-off black makeup patterns like the eyes of women in Egyptian tomb murals. She was wearing a black turban and a red caftan with mirror chips sewn into embroidered eyelets around the yoke. She was pretty striking. He liked her. He sat down and paid. The chair was perfect. He was going to prolong this. There was some colorless bright stuff on her lips that looked good. He was comfortable. She reminded him that she needed his palm. There was a tremor in his fingers. His hand calmed down right away when she took it. He admired her for staying in character. He could rest. She was value for money, just for her getup.

His mind drifted while the woman studied his palm. Friendship was a problem in the foreign service—having the kind of friend you could go to for comfort and advice. It was only natural to hold back when everybody you met would be moving on to some other country in two years at the outside. On top of that, potential friends were always one of two things—superiors or subordinates, neither of them good categories of people to expose your troubles to. Life was brief, really brief. And, if on top of everything else your wife was your enemy, good luck. He wanted to knock wood about having Lo.

He remembered another thing about Ione. She knew Setswana. But he had heard that when she was learning the language, she had refused every female tutor assigned to her by the Orientation Centre, insisting on having a male. People had carried on about that. Now she was speaking.

She told Carl that she was picking up enormous stress, but she wanted to know if it made sense to say that the source of this stress was unusual in some way. He said yes. She asked if this stress was from something other than a person presently around him. To Carl, this meant the dogs. This woman was extraordinary. Something was happening to him that was undeserved, she said.

He began about the dogs. She stopped him and said she wanted him to know she had sensed a nonhuman source for his problem, as he could verify in what she had said. He told her more. She said that he was facing a threat but that he could be helped. Either she was a superb actress or she was really concerned and serious. He found her convincing.

He told her everything. She listened intently. When someone tried to come in, she got up and said she was closed. It was only someone reporting that the Brits had won second, anyway. She had him go over his situation again, repeating certain parts. She was intelligent.

Ione said she was going to help him.

That night he was still awake when the dogs began, at two. Things about Ione were agitating him. Why would all their arrangements have to be so sub-rosa? Why did he trust her? She was extreme.

He got up. Now that he was sleeping in the study, he had more freedom for quick, furtive acts of vengeance against the dogs: "venting behavior," Ione had called it, approving of it as a stopgap. He put on his shaving robe and went softly out into the yard. Next to the stoop he had a cache of small stones and fragments of roof tile. He hurled three stones in the direction of the worst noise. Two of his shots struck metal. There was no change in the barking. He felt better, less wound up, when he was back inside.

Also, he had never thought of Lois as tiny until Ione— trying to identify who Lois was—had asked if she was "that tiny blue-eyed person." Lo was small. Maybe she seemed smaller because of being with someone his height and also because she would never wear heels because of what they did to your spine. Of course, Ione herself was on the tall side, which would also explain what she'd said.

He was smoking again, a little, as a pastime and only at night. He felt it was justified. He lit a cigarillo. There was no inhaling involved. Lois would understand, when she found out. Dutch cigarillos were the best in the world, and they were cheap in southern Africa, for some reason. He would never be able to afford Ritmeester Seniors back in the U.S.

Ione put things in a way that stayed with him. He should imagine everything he'd done about the dogs, so far, as pictures in an album, with everything he had done in a certain category represented by one picture with a caption: a picture called "Lapidation" would show him throwing rocks through the fence at night. And the title of the whole album would be "Things That Didn't Work." And then he should believe that there would be a second album coming, with just one picture in it, and the title of that album would be "The Thing That Worked." But he had to believe in the second album. She had been shocked by his trapezius muscles, the rigidity. She had made him feel them himself.

He was getting more hopeful. The dogs continued. Idly, he began singeing the hairs on his wrist with the tip of his cigarillo.

Ione said, "I learned hypnosis from a fairly sinister woman—a religious charlatan, really. Classes in hypnotism were a sideline for her. Her main business was a little sect she ran in her garage, the Church of the Supreme Master." She was moving her hands in a smoothing pattern above him as he lay in a lounge chair. He was supposed to relax, but her insistence on meeting in the motel was still bothering him. She was sitting to his right, leaning over him. She had made him take off his shoes. Was it a sign that he was going under that he saw her hands almost as detached things? He asked her.

She said, "You have to try and avoid critiquing each step of the way or you won't go under. You have to let go more. Tell me anything that's still bothering you. I think you understand about confidentiality and so forth. I want to help you. Your situation is pretty severe. Go long enough with low sleep and you can begin seeing things, seriously. So I want you to seal all that up in a mental envelope and lick the flap and visualize it going into a mailbox. Concentrate on your tongue, licking. Good. That's better." She resumed her breaststrokelike movements. "Remember, we have plenty of time and you'll be back in your office by four, tops. I run a tight ship. You can trust me." He concentrated.

She said, "We met in her garage, where she had, I'll never forget it, a picture of Christ on the wall with the eyes coated with clear nail polish—to give you some kind of frisson, I guess. The other students were something. A woman who demonstrated stove polish in ten-cent stores for a living was one. And a man who at the time owned the largest sandblasting concern in New Jersey. He was losing contracts. And an unfortunate type who was in it for one thing only—the power to cloud women's minds. You follow me. She was a wonderful teacher, though."

Today Ione was normally dressed, except that her blouse had unusually deep armholes, if you were interested. She was wearing a tight white skirt and a white sleeveless blouse. She had started off by removing an ivory bracelet and her wedding ring, because they would distract him when he was concentrating on her hands.

She bent closer to him. "Think what I speak but don't move your lips," she said.

. . .

"This is sad," Ione said. Carl had the impression she was repeating herself. He had been asleep. "This is too sad, as they say here. You're too exhausted to be hypnotized."

He said, "I thought you were going to try again."

"I did," she said. "You only remember the first two tries, when I woke you up. The third time I just felt like I was torturing you. So I let you sleep."

It's just as well, he thought. His mind felt unusually clear. He hated the motel room. A brown line led down the wall from the air-conditioner to a rank spot in the rug. He felt a little panic. He was in danger. It was nearly four.

Ione was smoking. "We learned something from this," she said, soothingly, letting smoke out as she spoke. "We learned I have to catch you at the right moment—sometime when you've had a good night's sleep. Wait, I totally comprehend that that's exactly the problem, but wait for my plan. It isn't difficult. You need to spend one night away from the dogs and just sleep yourself out before we try this the next time. You have to travel, in your job. You could tell your wife you had some field thing to do. Do you know the Mafenya Tlala Hotel, in Molepolole?" She said this quickly.

Lois was young. She would never understand this. Hypnosis had been a mistake. Ione was saying that she still maintained he was a good subject for it.

He interrupted. "This is it for hypnosis, I think. It's not a good idea for me. I don't like the feeling, to tell you the truth."

She said, "But you haven't really experienced it yet, because you kept falling asleep."

He tied his shoes. He would leave first. She looked penetratingly at him, in a way that made him feel guilty and ungrateful. "I bow to what I hear in your voice," she said.

He said, "I appreciate your efforts."

A sliding door gave directly onto the parking area. The

drapes were drawn. "You can almost go," she said, looking out along the edge of a drape.

But he sat down. The idea of leaving was suddenly intolerable. It felt like a mistake. This was the only person who had tried to help him, except for Lo to the best of her ability.

He began apologizing. He said he'd felt from the beginning that hypnotism was going to be a no go for him. He apologized because he realized what he really wanted from her was probably a fantasy. His fantasy had come about because people said she knew all about the culture, and about witchcraft in particular. Probably witchcraft appealed to him because he was at the end of his rope. But wasn't there something to it? He thought she had been implying that there was, whenever they talked. He had seen birds kept off millet fields through juju, in West Africa. He knew the Batswana used witchcraft on one another. There ought to be some way to use it on dogs. He wanted her to admit that she had implied there was a tool available in witchcraft, the first time they'd talked, unless he had imagined it, which he admitted was possible.

She seemed to be going through some inner conflict, trying to persuade herself to help him. He said that he understood her position. He reminded her that he was desperate.

Finally, he sensed a reluctant decision in his favor. "I understand you," she said, seeming grave and hesitant. "But remember, I only know so much in this field. You could call me a novice. You want me to locate a *sangoma* for you— that's what you're asking." She closed her eyes for a moment. "Carl, you understand we'd have to be even more careful about getting found out than you can imagine. You know what it would mean if it got around that we were involved with witchcraft. And you would have to follow instructions, and I mean to the letter."

"Anything," he said.

. . .

Ione called him at work every couple of days to keep him current on her search for a *sangoma*. He found himself looking forward to her calls, which usually somehow evolved beyond the matter at hand to range over a lot of unlikely issues on which she had opinions he found interesting. His sleepless nights provided him with endless topics for discussion. Also, he liked her voice.

Again she was reporting no luck in finding a *sangoma*.

He said, "Stop looking if you want to. What really started me on this tack was when you said that some university had sent a team out to see if there was anything to the claim that *sangomas* could direct lightning strikes against certain people or places. I don't know. It gave me hope. When in Rome. But what a long shot! Maybe it's not a good idea. I get a lot of good ideas quote unquote at night while I'm memorizing the ceiling."

She said he was sounding defeatist. She went on for a while, trying to buck him up.

He said, "Here's another good idea that came to me, that I actually put some time into. It occurred to me that it would be funny to get up a fake memo saying AID should hereafter stop talking about the poor and instead refer to them as the 'pre-rich.' It was just for the bulletin board. This has to do with some incredible new reporting and nomenclature guidelines we recently got from Washington. I actually started typing this thing up the next day, before I realized what I was doing and tore it up. Close call."

She said she thought calling the poor the "pre-rich" was clever. She said his bright ideas should be thought of as insights.

"I'll give you another example," he said. "Answer this question. Do you like it in Africa?"

She said she did.

"But you can't quite figure out *why* you like it, am I

right?" he asked. "Because, I mean, hell, it's inconvenient.
Gaborone is dead at night, the movies are ancient and all
mutilated because they have to come through South African
censorship because that's where the distributor is located.
But still we like it here. Drought, poor people . . . Even
when they get a decent movie, they mix up the reels. We
want to be here anyway, but we can't figure out why. Except
that one night I figured it out. It's because it isn't our country
and we can't help what happens. We can offer people advice
and we get paid for it. We get good vacations, we eat off the
top of the food chain, we get free housing. Hey!, but we're
not responsible for what happens if Africa goes to hell, *because we've done our best.* Also, at the same time, we're not
responsible for what happens in America, either, really—
because, hey!, we weren't home when it happened. Say we
get fifteen per cent compliance on birth control here, which
is what we do get and which is terrific by Third World stan-
dards. O.K., *it's not enough.* But what can we do, we tried.
We told them. But *we're too late.* We all know it, but somebody pays us to keep up the good work, so we say fine. Why
am I telling you this? I forget."

She said, "What we have here are night thoughts—that
kind of thing. We all have them, Carl. You're very intelligent. You're excellent. I enjoy what you say. It's very O.K.
to have night thoughts. I find you really thoughtful. One
thing, though, is you might want to spare Lois this kind of
thing. I know it's important to share night thoughts, but Lois
seems so delighted about being here. Why cast a pall, if
she's really enjoying herself—do you follow me?"

"I'm not going to be a pall-caster," he said.

"Like broadcaster—oh, wonderful! I enjoy you," she
said.

He said, "Here's another example. Lying awake, I figured out the meaning of life one night. Not life in general,

but my life . . . what my life is about. It's about women. Women are the meaning of my life: taking care of them, looking for the right ones, trying to stay on their good side. The meaning of my life is the emotions women have about me. That is a fact. I think it's interesting. I was amazed. When did I enlist for that? I thought I was doing something else."

She said, "I want very much to help you. Let me pursue what I'm doing. Let me find someone, Carl. I'll get back to you."

He said to go ahead.

"Look!" Lois said to Carl, as he came in from work. She was elated about something. She stood there, breathing forcefully.

It was nothing self-evident. Was it a new piece of clothing or something from the sea freight that had just arrived? Her hair was the same as recently. He resented having to guess. He was already fully tasked. Also, there were echoes of Elaine involved—Elaine's fury the times he had failed to notice some crucial purchase or that she'd bleached her lanugo.

"Carl, I can breathe through both nostrils at once! Look, my sinus thing is gone one hundred per cent! It was just about four this afternoon. It's just *gone away*. I feel like I'm just flooded with air." Her eyes were bright and moist. It was important.

She embraced him a little fiercely. He was already elsewhere. His mind was back on his mission. Ione had found a *sangoma* in a village fifteen minutes from Gaborone—a *sangoma* who seemed to know all about how to deal with problems like the dogs. So Carl had been right. Ione was giving him credit for guessing there had to be some ultimate mechanism in the culture for dealing with unbearable situations—whether it was witchcraft or not. In the United States it would be the Mafia. Ione had been skeptical at first. Now she was excited.

Lois was being grateful, pressing against him. She was easing his shirttails out. He was getting the idea. Lois slipped off a sandal and rubbed her heel against his calf. I can do only one thing at a time, he thought. There was no time for this.

"Don't be so tired," Lois said, pleadingly.

But tonight he had to get a dog bowl from Letsamao's yard, somehow. He needed to plan. The *sangoma* had said to get hold of some object common to all the dogs. Carl needed to reconnoitre.

Lois was hurt. "You could at least put your briefcase down," she said.

He did. "I don't think you grasp how tired I am," he said. He was all apology.

She was badly upset. She was liable to go to the bedroom, which would be perfect if she would stay put there long enough for him to get outside and spot the last locations of the dog bowls before night fell. Then he could recoup with her.

Lo announced that she was going to lie down for a while. She was giving him another chance. The implication was that if he was as tired as he was saying, it would make sense for him to lie down along with her. He acted blank. She left. The bedroom door closed loudly.

In the yard, he wandered along the fence, pausing to pick bits of refuse out of the mesh. The dogs were dining. There was the bowl he needed. It was white enamel. When the dogs were through, the bowl was twenty feet from where he stood. He needed an instrument. He needed an instrument that didn't exist, except in comic books—a pair of monster accordion tongs. He would have to go over or under the fence in the dead of night. There was no other choice. It would be safer to go underneath. He could excavate in the guise of filling in tunnels dug by the dogs. A shallow trench would do it, something just deep enough to let him roll under the sharp bottom tips of the fence. Would he ignite the dogs when he got over there? He would have to see. He wasn't physically afraid of the dogs, except for the two ridgebacks. The dogs were cowards, basically. Pretending to pick up a rock would make them shy off. Even if they did bark, he would be there and back so fast there shouldn't be any danger. Also, the dogs knew him. And best of all, nobody at Letsamao's paid any attention to the dogs, whatever they did. It would be safe. He would wear heavy stuff on his arms and legs, and heavy gloves, just in case. He wound a twist tie around the fence wire at the point closest to the dog bowl. He was set.

This would be work. It was manual labor. He wouldn't mind it. The real beginning of the end with Elaine had been when he overheard her refer to herself as "labor" and to him as "management." Naturally, he had let her snake out of it, believing her when she claimed she was only calling him "*the* management"—a different thing. Then, during the divorce, it had turned out that calling him "management" was nothing—it was praise, compared to other things she'd said.

Everything tonight had to be kept from Lo. He was grateful it was Lo that things had to be concealed from, not Elaine. Elaine would have been a participant, because she would have found out what was going on. Elaine was temperamentally a Roman empress. And especially in her tastes—she had worn herself out trying to force her needs through the eye of a needle: himself. Lo wanted less than he could provide. And she was still economizing. He would have to be certain she was asleep when he struck tonight, like a commando.

In the garage he examined the spade he would use. If Elaine had been a Motswana, she would be the richest woman in the country. More Africans should be like Elaine. It was too bad there had been no way she could go into business for herself—for the wife of a foreign-service officer, that had been impossible. Mostly she had been able to get only trivial jobs, like doing property inventories or managing the commissary, except for the one job she had done everywhere and done magnificently—writing the post-differential-payment report. Her reports were masterpieces. She could prove that any foreign-service post in the world was enough of a hellhole to justify twenty to sixty per cent more income in the form of hardship allowances for all hands. Everywhere they had gone, Elaine had been given the differential report to do. Nothing escaped her: windy seasons so brief that no one else noticed them, cheese shortages, mildew problems, no dry cleaning, obscure local diseases lying in wait. The differential report had spoken to her genius at faultfinding. He could imagine what she would have done with the dog problem: she would have turned it into gold for the entire mission. She could take an earthly paradise like Blantyre and make it sound like Pompeii in its last ten minutes. People confessed things to her, like unreported rapes and embarrassing ailments. When she was in the presence of concealed information, she knew it. In fact, if he had ever missed two staff meetings in a row in Elaine's time, she would have known it and it would have meant cold meals, no sex—the whole works. It was bothering him that there might be some simple means of getting the dog bowl that would have been obvious to Elaine which he was overlooking. It couldn't be helped. Tonight he would be a thief in the night, like the Thief of Baghdad, which he had just realized was the best movie he had ever seen.

. . .

Carl attacked the ground. Botswana was sand. Lo was sound asleep, knock wood. Carl worked hunched over, trying to remain alert for any sign of activity at Letsamao's. His body felt light. The dogs were watching him. It was moonless, knock wood.

He felt partly brilliant and partly absurd. He was wearing war-surplus paratroop boots he had carted all over Africa and never used, a watch cap pulled down to his eyebrows, a black, wet-look windbreaker Elaine had insisted on buying for him in the Marais. He hated it. The only reason for buying it had been to enable her to name-drop the point of purchase. With any luck at all, he'd wreck the jacket in the raid tonight. He had to be careful about Lo's black mittens, though, and get them back unnoticed into her glove drawer. She was frighteningly well organized. In the right-hand pocket of his windbreaker, ruining it, was his secret weapon—lumps of raw beef to throw to the dogs to distract them. He had to get things over with because he was stifling inside his action costume, which was what it was.

The trench was too short. Until this moment in life he had always enjoyed being taller than anybody around. He should have hired someone to do the trench, like the street boys who washed your car behind your back and against your instructions and then demanded money. It hadn't occurred to him. He continued digging. The bottom teeth of the fence went down less than an inch into the soil, he had been happy to discover.

He lay down and rolled under the fence easily. The bowl gleamed at him. He stood up as a wave of dogs, muttering, rolled toward him. He flung the meat in an arc just over their heads, and they wheeled. It was like magic. He had the bowl! The dogs were after the meat, breaking up into vicious knots here and there. This was Letsamao's karma for underfeeding them. Maybe their whole problem was being underfed. He was back in the trench and rolling home. He stood up, shaking himself. He collapsed the lips of the trench and swept loose earth into the hole, enjoying everything.

He was curious to know why he felt physically light, so light. He felt almost removed from his victory, standing aside. It was amazing. What he had done was amazing. He had forestalled the dogs. He felt fine, he felt amazing. Everyone said forestall this, forestall that, but how many people knew the term came from rebel merchants setting up markets outside the authorized markets run by the barons and bishops and so on, in England? How many people knew it came from the history of marketing? England was conquering the world in the guise of her language. Poor devils here in Botswana had to abandon their own languages in order to get a degree. Suppose he'd had to learn German at a tender age in order to get anywhere? The people we deal with day in and day out are all linguists, he thought. He slipped the bowl inside his jacket, zipped up, and went in.

The phone rang. It was Ione, at last. He had been waiting for days. She got directly to money. It was two hundred pula. At the current rate, that would be about two hundred and fifty dollars. Then she gave him instructions. She was breathless. At the end, she said, "Carl, I want only one thing out of this, and it's fine with the *sangoma,* and that's to be present—be there for it. This is a whole new step for me. So, I'm hoping to God you have no objection. And also you owe me this. And it's a good idea for me to be there, just in general. And he understands absolutely about confidentiality."

He said he wanted her to be there. She was relieved.

The instructions were easy. He was supposed to be "clean in his person" and to wear clean clothes.

. . .

Ione was trying to modulate everything. Let her, he thought. As she drove, she was trying to keep him relaxed and positive. She was driving especially carefully, suppressing her impatience whenever she had to stop and get out to let them through cattle gates. She wouldn't let him help. She wanted him to rest, which was all right with him, because last night the dogs had been straight from hell itself. Ione had even brought a pillow for the small of his back.

There were a lot of mountainous clouds. She had pointed out some odd cloud forms. It was balmy. The little hills above Ramotswa were greener and more normal-looking than the ones he was used to—like the steep hills around Lobatse that looked like piles of rubble or cobblestones. Was she worried that he was going to back out, still? He smiled to himself. On his lap in a paper bag was the dog bowl. He was holding on to it with both hands.

Ione was following directions written neatly on an index card. These back roads were rough. He wasn't sure where they were, at this point. The last landmark he'd paid attention to had been a garage—a panel-beaters place near the main road, a good while back. He liked the way Ione dressed. Today she was wearing a long-sleeved khaki blouse and matching pantslike things whose name would come to him. Lo would look like a Brownie in Ione's outfit, but on Ione it was just right. Sometimes Lo bought clothes in youthwear. The only thing against Ione was her eyebrows, which were too thin and not in their original location. But that was nothing. He couldn't help admiring her calves as she worked the brake and clutch. She had muscular calves, like a dancer. Culottes, she was wearing.

They arrived. She seemed not to like the looks of the place, and told him to stay in the car while she scouted around. There was a mud-block storage building standing alone at the edge of a deep ravine. Where was this? They had come down into a valley with bad gully erosion everywhere he looked. The building was windowless. The roofing was motley—boards and sheet metal held down with stones. A line of elephant grass grew around one side and the back of the structure. There were no other buildings anywhere in view.

Now Ione was motioning him to come over. He got out. The entrance was at the back—a hole probably originally intended to receive a doorframe. The void was covered with a tarpaulin, which Ione pushed aside with a stick. Candles burned in several places inside. They entered.

It was difficult to see much. Where was his night vision? Something like a heap of rags in one corner rose up and walked. Ione jumped. Carl was steady. It was the *sangoma* approaching.

How usual was this? The *sangoma* was dressed in an assemblage of light and dark rags, pinned together, and he was masked. Toweling was wound around the top half of his head, ending just below the nose. The eyehole edges were ragged. A headband secured the toweling, and feathers hung down from it on one side. The *sangoma*'s arms were bare. There was nothing imposing about him. There was something sad. He looked frail. He seemed to be alone. The place had been neatened up in a rough way, the earth floor raked. There were ramps of earth and debris in two corners. Some penetrating smell hung in the air. There were sacks of something along one wall which could be sat on in a pinch. It was all right. He didn't love the ceiling beams, which were studded with white pods—some of them as big as doorknobs—which he knew were spiders' nests. He could make out a cot and a small table at the head of the room. He was ready anytime.

· · ·

Carl lay on the cot, waiting. First, Ione had insisted on checking the cot for stability. Then she had insisted on dusting the cot off with some tissues she had. Then it had been O.K. to lie down. And now she had run out to the car to get him the pillow she'd brought. She was taking more of a hand in things than anybody else present liked. There had been trouble over the money, when she made Carl keep half of it until the procedure was over. And that had led to the *sangoma*'s first request that she consider waiting outside, which she had resented. Now he had the pillow, and there was a compromise: she would sit on a sack at a reasonable distance from the scene of the crime.

The thing began, at last. He wanted to tell Ione to relax, and to remind her that there were such things as trade secrets and that from his standpoint, the *sangoma* was already being pushed around. This man was an entrepreneur, when you came down to it. Also, it was Carl's money, and so far he felt like he was getting his money's worth—some dance steps and swaying as the *sangoma* circled around him, some business with bones in a pouch, some pouring of liquids into and out of the dog bowl. How could she expect to be allowed to scrutinize everything? They weren't there to make a documentary. It was too dark for that, and this kind of thing was along the lines of a séance. He wanted to tell her that people didn't take flashlights to séances and sit there shining them around. Besides, a good part of the ceremony was going on behind a screen made from sacking. Maybe the *sangoma* hadn't liked Ione explaining at the beginning, over and over and over, in what would have to be called Basic English, what Carl's problem was and what the ritual was supposed to be putting an end to. From what Carl had seen during the money imbroglio, the *sangoma* spoke perfectly good English, although maybe that was strange. Carl was satisfied, was the point. The *sangoma* was humming. For a moment,

Carl felt he knew the tune, from South African radio. But that was impossible. He liked this thing. It went on.

Now the *sangoma* wanted him to turn onto his stomach. He complied. Ione materialized near them, enraging the *sangoma*. The old argument began again. Ione was interfering. This time the *sangoma* was obdurate. Ione would have to wait outside while he completed the ritual, which was almost at an end, and he would absolutely refuse to continue so long as she stayed. He appealed to Carl, saying "*Rra,* you must command this woman. She must wait some time on the outside, from this moment. She shall destroy my power." He had a hoarse, grating voice. He sounded weak. Maybe this was hard work for him.

Carl asked Ione to wait outside. She was unhappy. He said he would tell her everything that happened—that was a promise. Something was bothering Ione which she wasn't communicating, but there was no time for this. She wouldn't budge.

He was having to keep her face in view from a painful angle. This business couldn't be dragged out forever just because she didn't like some detail or other. She had had her chance to be an observer. The *sangoma* had to be allowed to finish.

She said, "Then are you, yourself, asking me to leave you in here?"

"I think I am," he said.

He had to shout at her, finally. It took his last strength. He tried to point out that they had paid their admission, that this wasn't like going into a restaurant and walking out after you looked at the menu. That had been Elaine's specialty. She loved doing it just a little less than sending food back to the kitchen, which would happen at any point in a meal, so that you were never safe. You were on tenterhooks every time you ate out. He shuddered.

The *sangoma* bent over him. "Thanks, that woman is gone. Now you must set this into your mouth." The *sangoma* handed Carl a piece of cardboard folded in half. Carl didn't like this, and now the *sangoma* was untucking Carl's shirt and pushing it up to expose his back. Carl wanted to say something, but the *sangoma* was chanting again, and the thought of interrupting seemed wrong. The *sangoma* gestured for Carl to bite down on the cardboard, so he did.

The *sangoma* bent down to him again. "Now what I must do is cut you some places, just like this way . . ." He dragged a thumbnail lightly along the canvas near Carl's face. "It is just your skin."

Carl started to get up, but checked himself, overcome by a new sensation. It was the sensation of conviction. The ritual felt real to him for the first time. Someone whose motives were good was going to reach down and cut him while he was wide awake. It was remarkable. He relaxed.

The pain of the first cut startled him. He had to concentrate. He counted the cuts as they came. The first was the worst—the deepest, he guessed. There were six cuts all told, three on each side of his spine, all on his upper back. It was like being burned. He gathered that the instrument was a knife blade, not a razor. He was breathing too fast.

"*Rra*, I must put you some powders," the *sangoma* said, tenderly. He patted Carl's neck.

The powder made his cuts sting even more. Carl spat out the cardboard. The *sangoma* tamped the powder down. Carl smelled ashes.

The *sangoma* helped Carl sit up. "You must set your shirt right," the *sangoma* said. Carl tried. His back was crawling with pain that had to stop if he was going to walk. The *sangoma* helped him with his shirt and then with finding which pocket the balance of the fee was in.

Carl got to his feet. He was all right. He could walk

decently. The *sangoma* would keep the dog bowl, apparently. The *sangoma* said something about not worrying anymore about the dogs. It was over.

Outside, it was brilliant. He kept walking. The air was sweet, overwhelming. There was Ione, pacing and smoking near the car. Now she saw him. She flicked her cigarette butt into the *donga,* which he wanted to stop her from doing because of veld fires, but it was too late.

The thing now was to get to the car. There might be some bleeding. If Ione noticed something, she would start up again with the *sangoma* and they could never leave. He thought, I have to keep my back behind me.

Once they were moving, she wanted to talk. He put her off, pleading fatigue. A taxi passed them, going in the opposite direction—unusual, because taxis mostly stuck to the paved roads. Ione slowed, craned her head out the window: clearly, she was trying to catch the taxi's plate number, but why? Something is eating her, he thought. He would hear all about it. He promised to be available at the office the next day for a leisurely phone call after lunch. That seemed to pacify her. She was concerned about him. He felt fine. He had done everything he could. There was nothing else. She was driving too fast. The jolts hurt his back. He was nearly faint.

They were still nowhere when Ione stopped. She wanted to know what was wrong. He told her about the cuts. He couldn't help it. She wanted to go back and find the *sangoma.* Her face was set.

He argued. He said the *sangoma* would be gone. He said it was getting too late. He told her she couldn't. He had to get home.

She listened to him, finally, and drove in the right direction.

· · ·

At certain moments he felt like a genius, or fox: only Ione knew about going to the *sangoma*. But he was sick. He was aware that he was fairly sick. His fever was up and his throat was bad. He was perspiring everywhere. But luck was with him. For months he had been warning Lo that everyone who came to Botswana got tick-bite fever sooner or later, which could actually be what he had, although he doubted it. Anyway, she accepted that tick-bite fever was what he had. His cuts were still his secret. They had to heal. Five of them had. The other part of the game was to keep the nurse from finding anything out.

He was getting sleep. He was taking sick days and sleeping all day. At night, if he heard the dogs they blended in with his fever dreams. They were still there. Lo was the best person to be around right now, because she distrusted doctors and loved taking care of him and would go along that way for time immemorial.

But then he was getting too weak. It was hard to really want to get well, because of the pleasure of sleeping. But he was getting too weak, for sure. So far, Lo was just giving him aspirin, because she was all gung ho for letting nature take his or her course, so naturally she was going along with the proposition that you just take aspirin for a week or so and let the tick-bite fever burn itself out and then you're left immune for time immemorial, instead of going for tetracycline which knocks it out in twenty-four hours but leaves you still susceptible. But now it was time to get well fast, so it was time to go for his secret weapon: Elaine's pharmacopeia. The glands in his armpits were hurting. Elaine always got doctors to give her their free samples of every damned thing. Elaine always had everything she might need for medication because she for one would never stand for being someplace in the Third World and finding herself where some doctor could say yea or nay. Somehow her medicine collection had wound up with his effects, not hers, after the split. So now it was his, all the Valium and all the rest. Why did he end up with it? He knew she had dynamite antibiotics in there. Why did he have her medicine? She must have forgotten. If she remembered, she might get a cable out on it. But now it was his.

He was having long dreams. It was always too hot. The walls were sliding up into the ceiling all the time. Lo was scared, he could tell. He was beyond food. Lo wanted the nurse. On the other hand, he would be all right any day because of Elaine. He was only tasting what Lo had given him—broths and so forth. It was too hot for broth. Lo was even letting there be air-conditioning. She loved him. He would be fine because of the neomycin he was taking—plenty of it. Elaine was saving him, Elaine, who got him going the first time they met by saying "Wreck me." Neomycin saved Elaine once. It was the strongest thing there was. He was young when she said "Wreck me." She knew what she was doing. Probably she was still doing it. Lo gave him a Compral to take. Compral was stronger than aspirin, and was from South Africa. He faked taking it. His eyes itched.

Before he could get better the nurse came, and then she was there all the time. She was gone, right now. They knew about the scabs on his back and were asking him about them. His throat was a good excuse not to answer things. He was keeping mum. He was worried about the knitting factory, because he was supposed to remind the women about something about business taxes. It was all right, because it was written down somewhere at work. He felt his hipbones by accident. They were like knives.

He was aware of arguments going on, but not really arguments. One thing he could tell was that Lo had been crying.

It was after the nurse found his neomycin. There was tele-
phoning to Pretoria. Now the nurse was giving him injections. Lo should be strong.

Ione woke him up, bringing him something, money, talking
too fast. She was talking so fast that powder was falling out
of the lines in her throat. He had a compress on his forehead.
She put the money in his nightstand drawer, and she was
whispering. She felt it was her fault about the *sangoma*, so
that was the why and wherefore of the money. She said she
had to talk fast because she had used a trick on Lois to keep
her out, so she could apologize—that was why she had to
talk fast. Some of it he understood. The *sangoma* was a fake,
just an actor jumping ship from a troupe from South Africa
putting on plays in churches in Botswana—morality plays.
He was an illegal person. She had been duped. She had
gotten suspicious when he was speaking English and
wouldn't use Setswana. Later on, she had realized he had
the same voice as the go-between on the telephone, when
she was searching for someone. And also, she found out
afterward that he had taken the whole thing out of a book—
it was Shona and not Tswana. She wondered if he had felt he
had to do the incisions partly because he assumed she knew
more about the ritual than she had. She was saying how sorry
she was. And then when Lo came, she changed the subject.
He felt sorry for Ione. He kept his hands under the covers.
He was better, he told her. He was understanding more. She
told him he looked like a carving.

Now he could get up all right. The world bounced when he
walked, but he could walk. It was going away with the injections. People were watching wherever he went. Lo was sleeping on her exercise mat at the foot of the bed. He almost
walked on her.

· · ·

He woke up with a mystery to solve. It had to do with the night before. The dogs had been active, and he remembered that clearly. But somehow he had slept hard at intervals while—he was sure—they were doing their worst. The answer wasn't sheer fatigue, because he was better. His tremor was fading. His appetite was back. Today he was going to read at least two back issues of *Finance and Development*, cover to cover.

Something told him the nurse was in the wings. He turned onto his side. He would pretend to be asleep, in the hope that she might look in and go away. Lo wouldn't let the nurse wake him up. He closed his eyes.

Bacon was what he wanted, but American bacon. That was one thing to be said about going back. Because it was clear they were going to have to go back. He had to stop fighting it. It was important not to panic over it. At least in America they put the lettuce inside the sandwich, not strewn in shreds all over the outside. Money was going to be the problem. He was afraid. People would tell him to go into business, leave the agency. He was an expert on business. But the idea repelled him. Why was everything in the world for sale, exactly? In fact, he was with the government because selling things seemed repellent to him. The government gave things away.

But nothing could be done. He was leaving Africa to her dogs. Lo would have to forgive him. Lo had worked before. She had been a cashier. She could learn bookkeeping—he would teach her. He had never taken one thing from Africa. This was too much self-pity. He had never touched an African woman, never, even when he could have. And when Elaine wanted to hide jadeite and tiger-eye in their household effects to smuggle back into the United States, he had drawn the line. He was through here. He was being destroyed.

Somebody was coming.

The nurse shook his shoulder. He rolled onto his back. Something was wrong.

"I've been talking to you," she said, but not impatiently. She was being kind. She had an instrument in her hand. Lo was with her.

Making a show of fatigue, he turned back onto his side.

He was beginning to understand something. He lifted and lowered his head slightly, blotting out her voice when he set his head down. He sat up violently, full of hope.

Lo was saying that the nurse had something to tell him. *He knew what it was.* The nurse said he had been septicemic. He had self-medicated and he shouldn't have. He had used something that was ototoxic and had made himself deaf in one ear, and she was sorry. Lo took his hand. She was weeping. The nurse was snapping her fingers to either side of his head, while he smiled. They could stay.

ALONE IN AFRICA

It seemed to Frank that he was adapting surprisingly nicely to life without a wife around the house. He wondered what it meant. By now, Ione was in Genoa or Venice or some other watering place in Italy. All her stops involved lakes or the beach. It was all there in the itinerary on the wall next to the phone. He could read it from where he was sitting and drinking, if he felt like it. He thought, Ione likes it overseas and she likes being here in Botswana, but the drought is wearing her down. The government was talking about cutting the water off from eight till dawn. It was going to be inconvenient for compulsive hand-washers, which he no longer was, but which a lot of other dental and medical people were. Ione felt parched, she said. So it was goodbye for three weeks. He toasted her again. There was a poet, an Italian, who had had Dante's works printed on rubber so he could read them sitting naked in a fountain with the water running over him: that was the image of her vacation she'd said she wanted Frank to have. So it was goodbye, because he had the dental-care design team due in from the AID office in Nairobi to praise his plans for Botswana's dental future, or not. There it was again, the small sound in the night he was trying to ignore. It was probably animal or vegetable. He was going to keep on ignoring it.

He'd be alone for another ten days. He was used to separations, but normally he would be the one traveling, not the one hanging around at home—which was different. Earlier in their marriage, and only for a couple of years, they had taken separate vacations. They had given it up after deciding they preferred to vacation together, all things considered. They kept each other amused. She was good at it. She was superb at it. He was missing her, especially on the sex end. He was enjoying being alone, otherwise. He was really alone, because the maid was away for a couple of days. Dimakatso's family was rife with deaths and emergencies. Women probably disliked being alone in houses more than men did because of routine small nonspecific sounds that got them keyed up. Right now he could easily convince himself that someone was horsing around outside, scratching the flyscreens. Ione kept him busy, sexually. She was six years older than he was, but no one would guess it. She had kept her figure to a T. She was sinewy, was the word. Ione had a dirty mind. In twenty years he'd never really strayed. She was a Pandora's box of different tricks and variations. Probably that was why he'd been so faithful. She was always coming up with something new. How could he feel deprived? Of course, the scene in Africa was nothing like Bergen County when it came to available women. Young things were leaving the villages and coming into the towns and making themselves available at the hotel bars for next to nothing, for packs of Peter Stuyvesant. It was pathetic. They wanted to get in with expatriates. They wanted to go to expatriate parties so they could latch on to someone who would buy trinkets for them or, if they were lucky, take them away to foggy Holland forever to get neuralgia. They wanted bed and breakfast for however long they could get it. The drought was making it worse, squeezing more and more people out of the villages all the time.

One guy he was tired of was the number two at U.S. Information—Egan the blowhard and world's foremost authority on sex in Botswana and the known world. Frank was tired of professional libertines, especially if they were on the United States Government payroll. Coming overseas had been an eye-opener on the subject of official Americans like Egan, who were less than gods, from the taxpayer standpoint. Egan was the mastermind behind the new thing of morale-building stag dinners for the men of America in Botswana. Frank had been once. No matter what you'd done, Egan had done it better. Somebody had made the mistake of using the phrase "naked broad." So then Egan had informed him he didn't know the meaning of the word "naked"— meaning that there was some elite whorehouse near Athens where all the women were shaved smooth as eggs. Their heads were shaved, their pubic hair, axillary hair, eyebrows. Egan had been there, naturally. The women were depilated every day. The women were oiled all over, shining, and they were different races. Only if you'd been there could you say you'd experienced lovemaking to a naked broad, had the real experience, like Egan. Egan was close with the bishop. He was a Father of the Year type. Actually, a loudmouth was the perfect choice for information service officer. What was a grown man doing showing Audie Murphy war movies to the Botswana Defense Force? Frank detested Egan, the hypocrite. Frank toasted the martyrs of science versus the church, like Giordano Bruno. There were others.

With its big block letters, Ione's itinerary was like a poster. You couldn't escape it. Ione's handwriting was showing no sign of aging. Frank wore glasses for reading and she didn't. His signature was less of a work of art than it had been. He looked at the radio. In less than a year they'd be back home where they could follow the destruction of the world by nationalism and religion in crystal-clear broadcasts on all-news radio. In Botswana, the radio was an ordeal, partly because they had never invested in an aerial. He was tired of waltzing around the room carrying the radio, trying to find the one crux of radio waves that would allow him to pick up something intelligible. The news would be about Beirut again. Beirut was religion armed to the teeth and having fun. He was tired of Beirut. Drinking this much was a change. It was fun. He was beyond his norm. Usually they never missed trying for the eight o'clock Armed Forces Radio news. Tonight he was going to skip it. Nine-tenths of the radio band in Africa was cockney evangelists. It was a shame that the minute the Batswana got literate they were engulfed in Bibles and tracts and fundamentalism, a nightmare. But he was going to take a pass on the radio because he was listening to something much better. It had rained hard, earlier, for three minutes. Now water was ticking onto the dripstones outside, a delicious sound and not long for this world.

He liked his worst bathrobe best, which was why he had dug it up from the bottom of the hamper. It must be after eight. Tick-tock, where was their clock? Except for Ione's African arts and crafts collection, there was very little in the place that would have to go back to New Jersey with them when they left. They could have a jumble sale for everything else. Basically, they were camping. This was a government house and they were living in it like campers: they dealt with the huge furniture as just another exotic thing to be made use of, like a strange rock formation. The government procured the furniture in South Africa. Ione liked to call the Republic of South Africa a "taste-sink."

They were camping. That was partly why they had done only the bare minimum on the grounds. The other part was to get at their intolerable neighbor, Benedict Christie, or as Ione liked to call him, Imitatio Christie. They lived in Extension Six, an enclave of upper-level civil servants, Batswana and expatriate. They were at the outer edge of the extension: raw bush began outside their fence on one side. Christie wanted every expatriate yard to be a model of husbandry, like his, with row after row of cabbages to give to the poor. Christie was useful in one way, because they could tell the time by him. He went to bed at nine-thirty on the dot. In Christie's house, only one room was ever lit at a time. He was a model of parsimony not to be believed. Even where people had fixed up their yards, Ione had never found the out-of-doors in Botswana that inviting. There were more lizards in the trees than birds. It was important to be alert about snakes. Ione had never adapted. Frank decided to open up the Cape Riesling they'd been saving. He went to get it. Coming back, he went through the house pulling the curtains shut on all the windows and pausing to listen for the sounds that had been bothering him. There was nothing much. He should check on the time. He chronically took his wristwatch off when the weekend came, locking it away. Not to secure it, but because he liked the symbolism. In the government houses, everything locked: closets, the pantry, dresser drawers, the credenza with his watch in it, all the interior doors. They had pounds of keys to deal with.

He was holding the wine in his mouth for longer than usual before swallowing it, for no particular reason.

Our suffering is so trivial, he thought. His thought surprised him. He wondered what suffering he was talking about, aside from being in need sexually, thanks to Ione, a minor thing and natural under the circumstances. He was in favor of her vacation. He swallowed his Riesling. Africa was suffering, but that wasn't it. He knew that much. Because a central thing about Africans was how little they complained. Whites complained at the drop of a hat. Africans would walk around for weeks with gum abscesses before coming in for treatment, even when treatment was next to free. People were losing their cattle to the drought, and cattle were everything. But the Batswana kept voting for the ruling party and never complaining. His point eluded him. He gave up. Occasionally it hurt him to think about Susan, because in a way he had lost her to superstition, to Lutheranism. If you told anybody that, they would think you were kidding, claiming to be suffering over something trivial. They would say you were overreacting. His daughter was a deaconess, the last he'd heard. That was up to her. What was a deaconess?

He drank directly from the bottle. He liked the sound of liquid going into him. He thought, It's easy to forget how remarkable it is that every member of the male race carries a pouch hung on the front of our body full of millions of living things swimming into each other. He cupped his naked scrotum to see if he could feel movement. He thought he could. The wine reminded him of Germany. Everybody should see the Rhine. But when he'd suggested it, Ione had said she hated Germany. So did the Germans, apparently, who were ceasing to reproduce—voting with their genitals, so to speak. Germany was green and beautiful. So why were the Batswana reproducing like Trojans in their hot wasteland of a country? Fecundity was everywhere. Women began reproducing when they were still children. Everywhere there were women with babies tied to their backs and other babies walking along behind them. At thirteen or fourteen they considered themselves women. Batswana schoolgirls looked like they were getting ready for sex from menarche onward. They went around with the back zippers on their school uniforms half-undone, their shoes unlaced half the time, as if they were trying to walk out of their clothes. They were always reaching into their bodices, was another thing, feeling and adjusting themselves. They were unselfconscious. He wondered if they knew what that kind of thing looked like to *makhoa*? Batswana men didn't seem to notice it. He reminded himself not to judge. Women in general were a closed book, Ione excepted. And women in somebody else's culture added up to two closed books. What could a *lakhoa* really know about the Batswana, especially the women? A lot of things were said about them that were probably lies— for instance, that they had enlarged labia because their mothers encouraged them to stretch them as a sign of beauty. That was in the north. Probably it was no longer done. It was called macronympha.

It might be a good idea to eat. He was getting that feeling of elevation in the top of his head, from the wine. The top of his head felt like it was made out of something lighter than bone, something like pumice. He went to the window. Christie was having dinner. His kitchen light was on.

What were Christie's secrets? He was an elderly Brit, a bachelor or widower. It was no fun living next door to Christie, with only a wire fence between them and both houses on narrow plots. Frank thought of the time he and Ione had gotten into a mood, acting stupid, slamming doors on each other. One of them had slammed a door on the other by accident. Then the other had taken the next opportunity to slam a door back. It had escalated into slamming doors all over the house, a contest, and both of them laughing like crazy. So it had been slightly hysterical. It had been leading to sex. But then, naturally, the next thing they knew Christie had come out of his house to stand at the fence and stare in their direction, a gaze as blank and pitiless as the Sphinx, or as the sun, rather. Christie was left over from the days when Botswana was Bechuanaland. He was with the railway. He had applied for Botswana citizenship, which was tough to get these days. Probably Christie hated the idea of leaving the perfect medium for inflicting his religion on people to his last gasp. Christie's religion was restriction: no drinking, no smoking, no sex, no dancing. That was the real business of

the Scripture Union, which Christie was upper echelon in.
Christie was at home too much, was part of the problem. He
even held prayer meetings at home, endless events. Christie
seemed to hate Ione and vice versa. There was serious bad
blood there. Christie had his work cut out for him if he
thought he was going to make a dent in whoring. Whoring
was poor little bush babies coming to town to work as domestics and lining up outside the Holiday Inn at night to
better themselves. It was upward mobility. Visiting Boers
were good customers. Ione liked to use the stereo. When
he'd mentioned lately that when she played it she seemed to
be keeping it very low, they'd both realized it was an uncon-
scious adaptation to Christie, their monitor.

Frank could eat or he could take aspirin and drink some
more. He drifted toward the kitchen. Tomorrow was Saturday. The sound was back. There was really someone at the
kitchen door. There was deliberate tapping, very soft. Sometimes Batswana came to the door selling soapstone carvings
or asking for odd jobs, and their knock was so tentative you'd
think it was your imagination.

Frank moved quietly through the dark kitchen. He lifted
the curtain on the window over the sink. By leaning close to
the glass he should be able to make out who it was on the
back stoop, once his eyes adjusted.

It was a woman, a young woman. He could see the whole
outline of her skull, so she was African. She stood out
against the white mass of the big cistern at the corner of the
house. Her breasts were developed. She was standing close
to the door in a furtive way. He reached for the outdoor-light
switch, but checked himself. What was happening?

The key to the kitchen door was in a saucer in the cup-
board. If he put the outdoor light on it would advertise her
presence to all and sundry. She didn't want that, was his
guess. This could turn out to be innocent. He was ashamed.

There was no key. He calmed down. Was she still there? She must have seen his face at the window. He was feeling for the key on the wrong shelf. The keys should be kept on a hook so this would never happen again. He had the key. He set it down. He could still stop. He retied the sash of his bathrobe.

It was science the way he got the key into the lock in the dark and swung the door open silently, lifting it on its hinges. Before he could say anything, she had slipped into the kitchen, holding one hand open behind her to catch the screen door as it came shut. He closed the door. This was all so fast. He was having misgivings. They stood facing one another. He could hear that her breathing was agitated. He needed a good look at her. He pressed his hair down behind his ears. He was overheated. So was she. Somebody had to say something.

He turned the ceiling light on. For once, he was grateful that only one of the two fluorescent tubes was working. The less light and sound the better. She was beautiful. He studied her in the grayish light. She was beautiful.

She was looking down. Somebody had to talk. She was wearing a dark red wraparound skirt and a faded blue T-shirt open along one shoulder seam. She was barefoot. She would have some kind of pretext worked out. What do you want? was what he wanted to say, but he had to fight back his Spanish. He was almost saying *Que quiere?* He knew some Setswana, more than the average American expatriate. But his Spanish was welling up. She was still looking down. This was something that happened, but in bars and around bars . . . parking lots. How old was she? At fifteen you were a woman, or fourteen, or less. The crown of her head came about to his chin. She wasn't small. She had to be at least sixteen.

She looked at him. She was familiar. He searched his memory. He had seen her around. Every property in the extension had a back house, for servants' quarters. The back houses were meant for one family apiece, but the reality was that each house was like the Volkswagen with a thousand clowns coming out of it . . . endless children, relatives, transients. He associated her with the place three houses down. She lived in quarters. He had noticed her. She was a beauty. They were a family of daughters. The mother was a hawker. There were several daughters. This girl was the eldest.

She wasn't saying anything. What was he supposed to do? He concentrated. He had to get her name. He thought, Asking a name must be *O mang?* because *O kae?* means "You are where?" and *mang* means "who." People said *O kae?* when they met, all the time. The correct reply was *ke teng*, meaning "I am here." He would try *O mang?*

"*O mang?*" he asked. His mouth was dry.

"*Dumela, rra,*" she said. He had forgotten to greet her.

"Ah, sorry," he said. "*Dumela. O mang?*"

"*Ke Moitse,*" she answered, barely audibly, but clearly understanding him.

"*Ke Rra Napier,*" he said, pleased with himself. *But where was her mother?* He had overlooked something even more important than getting her name. What was the word for mother? *Rra* meant Mr. or man. Mother might be the same as the word for Mrs. or woman, which was *mma*. His bathrobe was embarrassing.

He said, "*O kae mma?*"

Now she looked baffled. "*Ke teng, rra,*" she answered uncertainly.

She didn't get it. This was a mess. It was like knitting with oars. He would have to go pidgin.

He was urgent. "*Mma* . . . is . . . *kae?* . . . your *mma.*" He pointed at Moitse for emphasis. Still she didn't understand.

Then he remembered: he had to say *Mma Moitse* to show

who he meant. That was the way it was done. People identi-
fied themselves as the father or mother of so and so, their
firstborns. He had to assume Moitse was the firstborn.

"*Mma Moitse o kae?*" he asked.

She understood. "*Ehé, rra.*" He was elated. *Ehé* meant
"yes," "O.K.," "now I see," and so on. She continued. "My
mother is to hospital. She is coming this side Tuesday week."
She was full of surprises. She knew English. She probably
liked it that he had tried Setswana. So far he was being a
fool. But the coast was clear. It was a relief and a plus that
she could speak English.

She had perfect skin. She was looking at him with a half-
smile, her chin held high. She said, "It is just because the
mistress is gone from you, and Dimakatso gone as well. So
you must say I may cook these days." But she was making
no effort to convince him that this was a genuine proposition.
She was trying to look brazen. Her expression was lasciv-
ious, but a child's version of lasciviousness, her eyelids half-
lowered, her smile studied. She was obviously a spy. She
had watched for Ione to be away, and then Dimakatso. She
had been watching the house like a little spy.

He said, "So, you want to be my cook."

"*Ehé, rra.* I can cook."

Her hair was elaborately worked in tight, ridged plaits
running straight back from her brow. It struck him that he
had an obligation. She might be hungry. He knew what was
going on. But he was not going to be put in the category of
bastards who exploited somebody's hunger. She had to be
fed. He wasn't going to be a bastard. She was here about sex
and they both knew it. If she still felt like it when she had a
full stomach, that would be one thing. They were both
afraid.

He said, "Well, so, but are you hungry, to eat now? *Dijo?*
Food? Do you want to eat, *kopa dijo?*" He knew he was
showing off.

She nodded. She was hungry. He motioned her to sit at the table.

He liked having a task. It would steady him. Maybe it would end the whole thing. The shepherd's pie was finished. He found a bowl of raw sugar peas in the refrigerator, waiting for somebody to do something with them other than himself. Canned soup was an idea. He found a can that looked appropriate. It felt heavy. According to the label picture, it was split pea with frankfurter slices. It should be nourishing. It was imported from West Germany. The instructions foiled him. Did he add water or not? He needed his glasses. He would add some milk. Did Moitse represent some kind of trap? He got the soup into a pot and filled a tea kettle. She could destroy him. But who would want to trap him? He had no enemies in Africa, just as he had no friends: he was passing through. He was in Africa to help. His presence would be reflected in people's teeth for years to come, assuming AID Nairobi said yea instead of nay.

He stirred milk into the soup. He would prefer to know her age. But she would only lie if he asked, so he would forget it. He could have been made a fool of, trying to get her age in Setswana. He thought, Thank God I didn't try. Numbers in Setswana were hopelessly complex. Ione made a joke about numbers in Setswana, which went How do you say ten thousand in Setswana? The answer was You say *bobedi* five thousand times. *Bobedi* meant two.

There could be some small talk about her cooking for him, while she ate. But beyond that, she had to make the first move. He had certain scruples. He hoped she realized that. Excitement was his enemy. So far, he was doing nothing wrong. He was making her something to eat because she was hungry, that was all.

The soup was swelling up. He had used a pot without a handle, something that looked like it came from a Boy Scout cooking kit. It was Dimakatso's. She used it for boiling mealie. There was no potholder in sight. He stared at the foaming soup. Moitse ran to the stove and deftly shifted the pot to a cold burner with her bare hands. Bravo, he thought. She stood close to him, smiling. She was slightly unfresh. Her nipples showed like bolt heads through the T-shirt cloth. She went back to the table. She had the usual high rump. Her hem went up in back. There were traces of mud on her ankles and a few smears of mud on the floor tiles. He was eating too much lately. He was overweight. He regretted it.

He grasped the pot through the cuff of his robe and poured most of the soup into a bowl. He brought it to her, then got out bread, silverware, margarine, and chutney. He couldn't find the marmalade, but chutney was in the same ballpark. She seemed to appreciate the need to keep the sound level down. She was taking his cues. The house was an echo chamber because they had decided to forget about getting rugs. Moitse asked for salt. He wanted his breathlessness to stop. One reason the stereo always sounded so loud was because the house was an echo chamber. Christie had called them up when they were listening to Manitas de Plata. Ione had been furious, because there was no point in playing flamenco except up high.

Moitse was catfaced. She had a small jaw, but perfect occlusion. Would she want money? He had nothing smaller than a twenty, he realized. She would be ecstatic. It didn't matter, because there was never going to be a sequel to this, never, so it wasn't going to be a precedent. Ione would be back. He wasn't seeking this out. She was oversalting. Being sought out made it different. Every human being had a right to a certain number of lacunae in his conduct. His glass was empty. He got up to refill it. Should he offer her wine? Yes and no. Not doing it was saying he was making a distinction—youth and age. It would be saying she was a child, which was far from true. On the other hand, if she was going to go through with this, it had to be out of her own free will not clouded by him. He was not going to induce anything to happen here. He sipped his wine. He brought her a glass of water. Tea was coming.

It would have been friendlier to offer her some wine. It might spoil things, that he hadn't. She was just looking at the water. She could be having second thoughts or regurgitating the Ten Commandments or her catechism, like a posthypnotic suggestion. The fastest-growing part of any denomination was always in Africa. Africans were Bible fodder, or *canon* fodder was better yet. He was going to have to remember that for Ione. It was clever. He had a dream. It was to run a gigantic work camp for preachers and priests and proselytizers who were going to be told to work for a living, in his utopia. The Catholics were going to have to run homes for surplus children forever, that was settled. There was a stupefying amount of religion going on. It was the Counter-Enlightenment. But what was he doing about it? But what could one individual do, especially in Africa?

He sat down opposite her. He liked the way she ate. She was neat about it. There was a little more soup, if she wanted it. But when that was gone they'd be in the lap of the gods. It would be the next stage.

She was a lynx, he decided, or a vixen. She started to clear up, nesting her bowl in the pot along with the silver. It was too noisy. He took over.

There was another inflaming smile out of her. She was inflaming him. He was losing his grip on the dangerous part of this, the complications, which he shouldn't. The exit signs were going dark. One thing was that she would have to wash first.

He was at the sink. She was behind him and then up against him, hugging. This was it, then. Her arms were around him. She was strong. She was brave to do this. She was holding him so hard he had difficulty turning around to face her. He put his arms around her and kissed her forehead. He was sick with fear and pleasure. He let himself stroke her breasts. The thing was to get her into the shower but to make it seem like fun, a plus, not an insulting suggestion. Asking her to brush her teeth would be too extreme.

"Moitse," he said. "Do you mind having a shower, with hot water?"

She seemed hesitant. He thought of miming what he meant. She might not know about showers.

He said, "You can wash your body, Moitse."

"*Ehé,*" she said. She didn't mind.

He led her to the bathroom. At the doorway, he stood aside, pointing to the shower stall. Still dressed, she stepped into the stall and pulled the curtain shut behind her. He turned the bathroom light on. He waited. There was no sound from the stall. Was it possible that this was her first time in a shower? The back houses had showers, but cold-water showers only. He should go and turn out the kitchen light. He had to be careful about lights and curtains to keep the place from turning into a peepshow. Ione's theory was that Christie had seen her naked once or twice, before she'd started being hypercareful about the way she walked around, before she'd realized what Christie was. Her theory was that Christie had never gotten over the shock and never forgiven her.

Back from the kitchen, nothing was changed—except that her clothes were in a neat pile on the window ledge. He pulled the shower curtain halfway open. She was naked. She was stiffly posed, her face tilted up at the showerhead, her eyes closed, her arms folded across her breasts. She was expecting him to operate the shower for her. It was touching.

He put his hand on her shoulder, guided her to step back. He could hardly think. He turned the water on, a tepid flow and not forceful. He handed her the soap. But she wanted to stand and enjoy the water: she held her pose, letting the water break directly on her upturned face. She was so calm. He wanted to touch her again. He was shaking, naturally. He touched her hip and then patted her mons. Her pubic hair was coarse, as he'd expected. "You must wash all around here," he said.

She nodded, but handed the soap back to him. She was going too fast. She lifted one foot onto the sill of the stall and torqued her body a little, thrusting her mons at him. He shied. He said, "No, you must do it yourself, but make everywhere clean. Stay here until I come back." He had to get away from her for a minute.

He returned to the kitchen. He was the one who was supposed to be in control. This was not the kind of thing that was going to happen to him every day of the week for the rest of his life and he wasn't going to be rushed and pulled down in the corner of the shower and so goodnight. His cuffs were wet. If this was going to happen, sobeit, but it was going to be with reasonable amenity and taking an amount of time worth the risk he was running. He diluted his wine with tap water. He washed his hands. He cooled his face.

The girl was some kind of veteran, so there was no virginity issue. The interest in virgins was pretty much a dead letter, was his impression. He was half erect. It was embarrassing. He tried deep-breathing, which helped. He heard the shower stop.

Moitse was standing in the stall, a towel wound around her head in a cowl. "We have to dry yourself," he said. He was mixing things up. He could hear he was trying to sound like someone in the media.

She came forward a little. He took a towel from the rack. Reaching into the stall, he dried her shoulders and trunk.

He caressed her breasts through the towel, briefly, teasing himself. He knelt on the sill and dried her legs. He pulled lightly at her right knee, to get her to uncock her leg so it could be lifted. He had to check for danger signs—lesions, scarring, rash. But it was all standard and clean. She looked down at him from beneath the cowl. All his associations for the way she looked with the cowl were religious. He wanted to lean his cheek against her belly, but he decided against it. Her foot was as hard as wood. He got up. His penis was erect. He tried to rearrange himself. She laughed and reached into his robe, grasping his penis at the base. It was painful. She pulled herself against him. She was too rough. He was speechless. She shook the towel off her head and tightened her grip. Shock gave him strength: he caught a tuft of her pubic hair and twisted it. She was going too fast again. She released him. He fell back and stood against the wall. She liked to play rough. He wanted to do all kinds of things, then. She knew how to play. She was back in the stall, standing there like a shadow. He had to think.

He needed a condom. That was next. He thanked God Ione was a varietist who came up with fantasies that involved condoms. How many guys with postfertile wives would have condoms lying around for an emergency like this? So now he had whatever was left of the rainbow pack. And that would be the couple of red ones, a magenta and a blood red, the ones he hadn't used because he felt they were subliminally frightening. They were in a hiding place in the linen closet, safe and sound. He needed a condom. There was no way he was going to find himself in the position of Peace Corps studs coming moping into the medical office saying they'd knocked up a local because there was no way they could resist when the women said condoms were insulting. Then there was the story he was trying to forget, about another Peace Corps character who had gone back to the U.S. leaving some village girl behind, pregnant. A child had been born. Other volunteers heard about it and collected money for the mother. Later they'd found out part of the money went for a special ceremony by a witch doctor, with all-night chanting. And the point of the ritual had been to get the whiteness out of the baby, let it be black. He told Moitse to go into the bedroom. He went to get a condom. Red was what there was.

He had a moment of fake fear. He was afraid there were no condoms where they were supposed to be. Fake fear was a juvenile thing he indulged in now and then. He would let himself fear something he knew was fake, and then be reassured—like letting himself think the car was stolen when he couldn't find it on the first try in the parking lot at the Paramus Mall. Maybe Ione had thrown out the red condoms. There had to be condoms because he was not a Boer or a fool and he wasn't going to impregnate anyone or pick up a disease. Also he should eat something, some protein, for strength. He needed something quick. He took the magenta condom from its hiding place.

In the pantry he found a jar of *sprinkleneute*, nut fragments for use in baking, which he more nearly drank than ate. He chewed violently. Afrikaans names for things always made him laugh. In the Republic, menswear was *mansdrag*. Drinks were *drankies*. Moitse would be in the bedroom now. He was chewing his best.

The hall light would have to be adequate. He doubted that Moitse would care either way about light versus dark: she was young. Ione was a good sport about leaving the lights on during sex. He was wearing the condom.

He got a surprise. Moitse had straightened things up in the bedroom. She had picked up his shirts and hung them on a chair back. His shoes were lined up under the dresser. She had tightened the sheets on the bed and was lying there dead center, a towel under her buttocks, a pillow on either side of her head, the blanket rolled down into a cylinder across the foot of the bed. She was still naked. Her clothes were in a bundle next to the door. She was lying with her knees raised, a little apart. With one hand she was lightly gripping her left breast, forcing the nipple up between her fingers. It was erotic. She seemed to be smiling. Her left hand was flat at her side, with something in it—a pad of toilet paper. The woman was a locomotive. This was not his style, but it was effective enough.

He got onto the bed, on her right. Some pleasantries would be good, but his mind was blank. He leaned on his fist and looked at her. The idea was to introduce the idea of taking it easy and appreciating things as they happened. But she let go of her breast and drove her hand under his hip, trying to lever him up and over her. His cheek slipped off his fist. Her strength was a shock again. She was using her nails. He rolled away from her, to think. In this format they were going to skip the kissing, apparently. At the movies, the Batswana laughed at kissing scenes. The stalls laughed and the whites in the balcony were serious. The good news was that she'd seen the magenta condom and hadn't blinked.

Now it looked like she had a new idea. She was covering her breasts with her hands. She was going to make him fight for her breasts. He lay against her and kissed her shoulder and neck. She drew her shoulders in. Either she disliked what he was doing or she thought it was funny. He was going to keep on. He was burning.

They heard a voice. Both sat up. She was rigid, listening. The voice was just outside, near the bedroom window.

"*Tututututututu,*" came to them, trilled softly.

"What is this?" he asked Moitse, his voice hard. It was someone imitating a bird, but why? It could be a signal of some kind. He was in danger. He could feel danger. He repeated his question, but more roughly.

Moitse put her hand over his mouth and shook her head, commanding silence, while she concentrated.

"*Ninini . . . ninini . . . ninini . . .* " This was a second voice, different, more piping. There were two people outside.

Then both cries were uttered in unison, followed by muffled laughter and scuffling noises. Moitse hissed.

I have to escape, he thought. He could get in the car. But that was irrelevant. He told himself to start functioning.

"I must thrash them!" Moitse said. She was glancing wildly around, looking for something, probably for a weapon. She leapt up and started pulling the belt out of a pair of his slacks. She was pissing steam, to quote Egan. He went to her, to control her. He got her by the wrists. She dropped the belt.

"It is my sisters!" she said. All this had nothing to do with him. She pulled against him, jerking her wrists downward with all her strength. "They are just teasing after me," she said.

The cries were repeated, more boldly.

"You're *naked,* what can you do?" he said. Number one, she had to dress. That seemed right. They were near the door. He let go of one wrist in order to reach for her clothes. She broke away, down the hallway to the kitchen.

"Relax," he said aloud. He felt his pocket. *The key was still in the back-door lock.* But she had to be kept in the house or Christie might see her running around naked if he was looking, if she got outside. Frank ran to the kitchen. This is why motels exist, he thought.

She was turning the key. He heard her say she was going to thrash them to hell. Then she was out in the night. He felt exhausted.

Outside, she was beating them. He could hear it. He turned out the kitchen light and waited. He stood in the open doorway, listening. He could lock her out, but he couldn't, because he would never see her again, and also he had her clothes. He wondered what Egan would do.

Someone small burst past him, knocking against his leg. He turned a stove burner on for light. There was a child under the kitchen table. She was badly frightened, judging by her breathing. She had to be gotten out, pronto. He crouched down to look at the huddled child. She was about six. She was shaking. She had bits of cloth in her pigtails. He stood up and patted the tabletop. "Relax," he said, as a second child burst into the kitchen. Her sister under the table called to her. He tried to catch her, but now both children were under the table. The new one was a little older. They were more ragged than Moitse, even. Moitse strode in, closing the door victoriously. The air was full of furious breathing. He wished he could laugh. The house was full of company.

Moitse was hissing Setswana at her sisters. Something was making him weak, other than being a little tight. He wished she would stop or continue indefinitely, because there was something about the moment. It was hellish and the best at the same time, with the light from the burner the only light and shining on her naked skin, her back, the cusps of her spine, as she bent down cursing her sisters. What was the name of the bone like a beak at the base of the spine? The sacrum. He was having a certain kind of moment. It was a little like being alone in the woods when a log or rock looks like a living thing for a second.

Now she was using English. "If you go from under this table *moonmen* shall find you and eat you to dust and spit you down from their jaws." She was terrifying them. He wasn't certain, but she seemed to be spitting at them to make her point.

He could probably dress her by brute force if he had to. He was a realist. She had to dress. The adventure was over. Moitse stood up.

He had learned one thing tonight: he should lock the door and hang onto the key. He did it. He put the key in his pocket.

He confronted her. She touched his chest. The gesture enraged him. He backed away. He turned the stove burner off and the overhead light on. He had to get some normality going.

She said, "They are bad. They are punishing me." Her eyes were moist.

"You have to get dressed *right now*," he said. "You must be dressed, fast. And then you must take your sisters home. Listen to what I say." He was speaking distinctly, he realized, like the Peace Corps schoolteachers he had met.

She pouted. She was going to be obstinate. The vamping look she'd used before was coming back. He couldn't believe it. She was going to argue.

"This is insane," he said.

"We can just go for that bed, *rra*," she said. "They shall stay this side, as a promise. Because I shall thrash them." She was pleading and defiant. She crossed her arms. She pushed her belly forward. That was seductive, he gathered.

He was desperate. He said, "You must dress very fast or I'll hit you. Do you understand me?" She was still being inappropriate. Her expression meant that she doubted him.

He looked around the kitchen for something to threaten her with, so that she would believe he would hit her. There was nothing except a wooden ladle. A wooden ruler was what he wanted. They were used to rulers from being punished in school, probably. There was one in the living room. Ione had used a ruler to make her itinerary poster. He went to look for it.

He drew the curtains on one window to let in a little starlight. He found the ruler. As he was reclosing the curtain, something alarmed him. Christie's yard light was on. That was unusual. There was also a light bobbing along the fence. It was Christie's flashlight. Frank was paralyzed.

He struck himself across the palm with the ruler, to make himself think. Christie might stop. He might stand around and see nothing and go back in. Or Christie might be on some errand that had nothing to do with him at all. He followed the light as it went out Christie's front gate and then out of sight, as it would if Christie were coming around from the street side.

What would Christie do if Frank sat tight and didn't answer? Christie was capable of standing outside the house until daybreak, when he could see Moitse and know everything. He was like a bulldog. There was no time. Or Christie was capable of calling the police, saying he was afraid something had happened if there was no answer. Or he could pound on the door, waking up the neighborhood. Frank was going to have to face Christie down and get rid of him.

He ran back to the kitchen. He took Moitse by the shoulders and told her there had to be silence, no talking, because someone was coming there. He shook her. Again he told her to dress. He told her he was ordering her to dress. It was hard not to shout. There was nothing else he could do. He had to get back to the living room and normalize.

He could weep at what he had gotten into. He was facing humiliation beyond belief. The living room looked acceptable. Something had to rescue him. Christie had to stop. Frank would be willing to do anything. He could lose Ione. He could lose everything. He was willing to pray, if Christie could be stopped. Christie could think twice and decide to go home. Agnostics could pray. God wanted belief in Himself, was the main thing—He wanted that more than vows to give up certain vices. If he could defeat Christie, he would be willing to say it was God's help that did it. Just the act of praying in itself implied belief. That should be enough for anyone. He thought, God, please save me, amen, this will never happen again.

He was a little calmer. There was no sign of Christie's flashlight. And then there was.

Delay would look bad. Christie was there, knocking politely but steadily. Frank opened the door.

Christie was no threat, physically. He was small, gray-haired, with a heavy, seamed face. He had pronounced lips. His dentures were primitive. Insects were swarming around the stoop light. Christie stood placidly in the storm of insects. Christie had a good baritone voice, an actorly voice. Frank felt a stab: he could have given Moitse the key and told her to get everyone out the back while he kept Christie busy at the front door. But instead the key was sitting in his pocket, reminding him of his stupidity. Christie was wearing black slacks, a dress shirt buttoned to the throat, and a gray foreman's coat. The effect was clerical. He was wearing sandals and white socks.

Christie spoke. "Good evening, sir. Might I step inside?" His tone was friendly.

"What's up?" Frank asked.

"Won't you permit me in, Mr. Napier? There are matters."

"You have a complaint?"

"Possibly so, yes."

"Then what is it? Just tell me."

"We'd best sit down over it, I think." Christie was being mild. Frank felt his self-confidence pick up. Christie was coming closer, like someone hard of hearing. Frank was encouraged. It was his house. But he needed a good reason for saying no to Christie, who was coming across like a member of the family.

"What do you say to tomorrow, Mr. Christie? I'm pretty tired tonight. In fact, I was dozing. . . ."

What was Christie doing? *He was walking in, almost.* He had his foot on the stoop and was inside the screen door, which had never had a lock. Where should Frank draw the line? Christie had his hand on the door and was pressing it, and Frank, slowly back—but smiling apologetically, it seemed to Frank, the whole time. Frank set his foot against the door, but the waxed floor betrayed him. Frank was divided. He was furious. But he was afraid that showing his fury would kill his last chance to manage Christie. He felt sick. The thing was to convert his resistance into the opposite. He opened the door to Christie. Christie was inside.

They stood facing one another in the dim coral light of the breezeway. Christie was upset too. This was costing him something. That meant there was hope. He was going to get out of this, thanks to God. He had to choose his words. He had to get Christie contained in one place, sitting down in one place in the living room. He wanted to batter Christie. But if he could get Christie sitting down, he could go to the kitchen for tea or Fanta or anything and get the key into the right hands and get his little friends out the back door. He had to let Christie see he was astonished at him but that he was honoring Christie's emotions, whatever they were.

"This is my house," Frank said. "So won't you come and sit down, since you're here." He was pleased with the way it sounded. He would usher Christie into the living room in the same spirit. He would disarm him.

But Christie was different now, all of a sudden. He was ignoring Frank. Christie was already in the living room, staring around, sweeping the room with the beam of his flashlight. Christie had to sit down: it was all Frank asked.

"Excuse me," Frank called out. "Would you mind sitting down for a second? You said you wanted to." Frank switched the ceiling light on.

What was Christie doing? Frank felt like he was always two steps behind Christie. God alone could control Christie. Frank would do more for God. Anytime the church came up, any church or sect, the stupidest, he would be silent. He'd go into radio silence until the conversation got around to something else. Christie was religion with the bit between its teeth, pushing into his house. Christie was Beirut.

He thanked God there was nothing for Christie to see in the living room. Christie was not sitting down. "I'll go get some tea," Frank said. There was desperation in his voice.

Christie reminded him of a lizard. He was quick. He seemed to be looking at something in the far corner of the room and then he was running for the hallway to the back of the house. He dodged past Frank. Frank felt betrayed. He reached for Christie, too late, stumbling. Frank was outraged. Christie would do anything. He would look under beds. Frank got to his feet and followed after Christie, his mind full of wordless pleading.

Christie was in the kitchen. Frank got there in terror. The scene amazed him.

It was brilliant.

Moitse, fully dressed, was sitting on a stool by the sink. She had a towel across her knees and the bowl of sugar peas in her lap. On the floor, sitting facing her with their legs straight out, were her sisters. They were watching her face fixedly. She was showing them how to string peas. Each of the younger sisters was clutching a handful of peas. There were little piles of strings on the floor. Christie was silent.

Moitse was speaking distinctly to her sisters. "You must just go this ways. I showed you about it. You must pinch this one that is thick, and pull around the top. The pea has a top, a back, like as if it is a man lain down on his face. So you must pull the thick one along the man's back. Then you must pull the small one along the man's stomach, where it is round." She demonstrated.

Frank was weak with relief. She was brilliant. He was

coming to life again. Strong vasomotor reactions swept over him. Christie was beaten. Frank could think. It was all over.

"Now you must clean," Moitse said to her sisters, who began sweeping up strings with their hands. "They are little, and we must go for home," she said directly to Christie, a little sadly.

"It's homecraft," Frank said. He was giddy. "She's teaching them homecraft. I said she could. It's nice for them. Why not? It's a nice thing. They don't have access to a real kitchen like this. So why not? Time to go, though, children."

Christie looked around at him, his face mottled, his expression intense but unreadable. He turned back to the girls, addressing them in Setswana. His first questions were in a gentle tone. Christie knew how to use his voice. Then he was impatient, and spoke sharply. He addressed questions to the younger two, but Moitse answered for them, angering him. She was hard. Frank could tell she wasn't giving anything away. She was hard as nails. He was in good hands with her. It was over. She was being sharp back to Christie. She was in charge. Frank unlocked the back door. One child's name was Gopolang. He wanted to talk to everybody, his relief was so great. That was dangerous. He was elated. He was feeling expansive. He could say too much.

"Remember to take the milk when you go," Frank said. He was improvising. He wanted to give everything in the house away, he felt so good.

"You must always listen to your sister," he said to the small girls.

He felt like talking to Christie. "You can always learn something, am I right? These peas. I always mangle them when I string them, you know? I learned something."

"It's past time they were home in bed," Christie said grimly, over his shoulder.

Frank said, "For sure. Time to get going. Better hurry.

They get interested and they lose track of time. My fault, because I dozed off in the living room." The two younger sisters went out, one carrying the milk.

Christie retreated to the kitchen doorway. Frank said, "If you want to talk about anything, we can. Maybe you'd like to apologize for charging in the way you did." Christie was self-absorbed. Would he say anything before he left? Frank let himself feel slightly sorry for Christie. He could patronize Christie. He wanted to hurt Christie, but he could afford to be understanding.

Frank wanted Moitse out fast. He was avoiding looking directly at her. She might reveal something. She was still a child, smart as she was. She was enjoying her victory. He motioned her to go. Christie could turn around and revert to his animal self, the way he'd been in the living room when he thought he had the scent. Moitse left. Frank locked up. He needed two hands to do it.

Now Christie was leaving. He was hurrying. Frank caught up with him in the breezeway. Christie had the door open already.

"You owe me an apology," Frank said. He was playing. He was toying with Christie. He couldn't let Christie go so easily.

Christie looked at him. "God is not mocked," Christie said, pronouncing God as "gaud," and using his most penetrating tone. "God led me here tonight. I go where He leads me. I am His servant. I have no apology to make. My pride to me is dust and rags. I am God's man. Good evening to you."

The house was filling up with insects. Frank shrugged. He said, "Goodnight, then."

Everything was too much. He watched Christie go. He wanted to see him back where he belonged.

A draft stirred Frank's bathrobe: out of the folds the

condom dropped, like a fallen blossom. It could have happened at any time in the last ten minutes. He stepped on the thing. He felt numb.

Frank went through the house and tested the locks on the doors and windows. It was a way of decelerating. He had to decelerate.

He went into the living room to watch Christie's house go dark again.

He went into the bathroom, where he took off his bathrobe and reburied it in the hamper. It was a rag and it smelled. He was ashamed. He would lie down and get up later for a shower.

He lay down on the bed. He felt his pulse slowing. Tears came to his eyes for a while. He was near sleep.

There was a scraping sound at the window above him, the sound of nails on the flyscreen. He recognized it. He sat up straight. She was back.

She was back.